STARLIGHT

Three riders emerge and savagely beat John Guiana. They steal three of his branded Lazy B horses, and when a battered Guiana rides into Cash's Crossing, Marshal Harding arrests him for bank robbery and murder. The thugs had used his horses to set him up — but why? Guiana slips out of jail, only to suffer a similar fate in Youngstown. This time he is rescued from a noose by Starlight line-rider Curtis Long. With the forces of evil closing in, Guiana must confront an enemy he has never met.

Books by Jack Sheriff
in the Linford Western Library:

BURY HIM DEEP, IN TOMBSTONE
THE MAN FROM THE
     STAKED PLAINS
INCIDENT AT POWDER RIVER
BLACK DAY AT HANGDOG
KID KANTRELL

JACK SHERIFF

◆

STARLIGHT

Complete and Unabridged

LINFORD
Leicester

First published in Great Britain in 2001 by
Robert Hale Limited
London

First Linford Edition
published 2002
by arrangement with
Robert Hale Limited
London

British Library CIP Data

Sheriff, Jack
    Starlight.—Large print ed.—
    Linford western library
    1. Western stories
    2. Large type books
    I. Title
    823.9'14 [F]

    ISBN 0–7089–9870–4

ULV   26. 7. 02

NE 6/8/02

Published by
F. A. Thorpe (Publishing)
Anstey, Leicestershire

Set by Words & Graphics Ltd.
Anstey, Leicestershire
Printed and bound in Great Britain by
T. J. International Ltd., Padstow, Cornwall

This book is printed on acid-free paper

Prologue

He was a powerful man and, seated proudly at the head of the long table flanked by members of his family, that power was evident in both the vibrant health and enormous strength of his huge frame and in the unquenchable fire glowing in the depths of his dark brown eyes that spoke of tremendous drive and willpower.

A crystal wine glass glinted in the soft glow of the lamplight as he lifted it to his lips. As he drank, he looked across the sparkling rim of the glass towards the opposite end of the table and met his wife's cold gaze. His own eyes were clear and untroubled in their nests of weatherbeaten, fine-lined flesh. He lowered the glass, and a hard mouth stained red with the rich wine relaxed into a smile and, in an unconscious, characteristic gesture, his hand lifted to

1

brush back his thick mane of white hair.

'You're planning something, Ben,' she said.

'Am I ever otherwise?'

'Oh, oh! Somebody out there had better watch out for trouble,' said the dark-haired young woman sitting on his left, and at once her mother shivered.

'I thought those days were gone. I thought . . . ' She shook her head, her lips compressed to a thin line.

'Position? Respect.' This was the young man sitting opposite his sister. Like her, he was dark, but the eyes that were mirror images of his father's lacked the bigger man's inner strength, and in the droop of the mouth there was petulance not firmness. 'Or should that be a certain reputation that comes mighty close to unsavoury notoriety, might even put a lesser man in the state Pen?'

'There's a dozen labels you could choose,' the big man said flatly, 'but what they all boil down to is the success that gave you an Eastern education and the rich living you enjoy.' He ripped the white napkin from the front of his shirt, scraped back his chair and stood straight and tall. 'I need to talk to Brad, share a smoke.' The hard tone directed at his son was unchanged as he looked at the woman who shared his life. 'Nothing of importance, Jenny; it'll take a few minutes, no more than that.'

A gnarled hand moulded by hard work brushed her shoulder as he strode past her; a faint smile curled his lips as he felt her stiffness, the almost imperceptible recoil from his touch. He planted a pearl-grey Stetson on his head, crossed the polished floor and went out into the night, pulled the door to behind him, heard the click of the latch and crossed the dark gallery to emerge from the shadows into pale moonlight. He waited by the rail, his eyes adjusting. Across the wide yard, beyond the barn and the first of the big corrals, a cigarette glowed. The big man reached to his shirt pocket, took out a fat cigar; lit it, blew a stream of

aromatic smoke, felt the sudden quick-
ening of his heartbeat and allowed
himself a thin smile.

It was a long walk across the yard
from the tall, spreading tree standing
in front of the ranch house, to the
log pile at the corner of the bunkhouse
where the man smoked patiently
in the shadows: a walk that was
another yardstick by which to measure
the awesome success that had been
achieved despite adversity, but which
was always tainted and soured by the
one wrong he had been unable to
right. Well, the time had come, the
wheels had been set in motion . . .

'They rode out an hour ago,' the man
in the shadows said. 'Be there by dawn;
move in so fast he won't know what's
hit him, then press on to the Crossing.'

'Who?'

'You know I ain't started takin' on
hands for the spring round-up. So it
had to be the 'breed, Sharpe Eagan,
Con Shipley, the wrangler, the useless
Mex you hired so's he could spend time

4

playin' with that Winchester and pickin' his teeth with a knife.'

The big man grunted. 'Tony Cruz. And what about Marshal Harding? Is he aware of what's going on? Agreeable?'

The man in the shadows chuckled, sent his cigarette sparking into the dust. 'Money talks. Hell, all you're askin' is he does his job — and I made sure he's got an angel watchin' over him in case he steps too far out of line.'

'Good.' The big man's voice was soft, the words now not for his foreman but for his own satisfaction. 'And then it's finished, at last, after twenty long years . . . '

His voice trailed away and, as he stared broodingly across the moonlit landscape that as far as the eye could see was his own land, one big hand lifted and fingers that trembled a little unconsciously traced the faded, V-shaped scar that encircled his neck and came to a high point under his left ear.

1

Three riders.

Beetles crawling steadily beneath the dark line of the trees, distance lending their approach an eerie silence, the sunless dawn light blanching colour from the mid-Texas landscape so that on the bleached grassland between river and trees they were nothing more menacing than three black dots.

And yet . . .

What is it that makes a man instantly wary, John Guiana asked himself? Why should three dawn riders tie a knot in his stomach, send his mind in the instant of sighting to the shotgun gathering dust on its iron hooks above the fire, to the still oiled, disused six-gun rolled in stiff canvas and buried deep beneath the dresses, delicate underwear and intimate mementoes Meg kept stored in the battered iron chest? And unable or unwilling to provide the answer, Guiana let the curtains fall and turned away from the bedroom window to pad on bare feet from the room where his wife, Meg, slept warmly with her hair a tousled mass darkening the white pillow.

He watched the riders for fifteen minutes, first from the front porch where he washed and shaved, stripped to the waist and wincing and shivering with the pull of the blunt razor and the shock of ice-cold water on his lean, sinewy frame; shortly after that from the yard — at those times when his line of sight enabled him to see between house and outbuildings — when he had pulled on his work shirt and boots and wandered from the corral to the sheds and back again with his mind only half on the day's work ahead.

'Damn!'

The big grey whinnied, drew interested snorts from the other horses, followed him friskily with nostrils flaring and tail cocked high inside the fresh-peeled poles as Guiana gave up the struggle to concentrate thought and, instead, strode past the corral to climb the knoll that was little more than a knob of rough ground at the south end of the property.

Closer. Not pushing their horses, but holding them at a steady canter. And there was only one place they could be headed.

But why?

No, he thought, and shook his head irritably. Not why, but why not? Hell, it was a free country. Hadn't he once, not too long ago, topped the south rise above this valley and let his wondering gaze rove wide in all directions, taking in trees and lush pasture and precious water flowing fast and deep as he marked a section in his mind? Hadn't he moved onto the land and lived with Meg in a lean-to shelter close to the woods while he built the cabin from pine logs, then felt the exquisite pleasure as time stretched endlessly before them and roots became established and the small spread expanded and its timbers were weathered by sun and wind and rain until one day he became aware that, like the soaring backdrop of trees, it was part of the landscape?

Eighteen months? Two years?

And now this. Jumping at dark, moving shadows. Seeing danger in the approach of mounted strangers, in the way they came riding out of the dawn — because, after all, hadn't that been the way he lived; the way, in times without number, he had come awful close to dying?

He heard Meg clattering pans in the kitchen, felt the nakedness of his hips as he walked hurriedly down from the knoll and the three riders rode up the long approach slope to the spread he had, from the beginning and with rich humour, called the Lazy B, now moving fast but almost soundlessly across the soft ground, weapons glinting at hip and saddle as the first dazzling rays of the sun slanted down from the mountains.

They swung in alongside the corral and their boots were already stirring the dust when Guiana was still thirty yards away, three armed men stepping down and away from their horses, drifting apart in an apparently casual movement that was nevertheless carefully orchestrated — and Guiana's mouth went dry.

'We're takin' three horses, feller.'

This was the man in the middle, tall, unshaven, sunken cheeks under the high facial bones of an Indian, dark eyes glittering and large teeth flashing in a savage grimace as gloved hands brushed the twin .45s suspended low on lean thighs.

After a moment's hesitation — after weighing the odds and finding them daunting — Guiana said carefully, 'Pick out the ones catch your eye, I'll name you a fair price.'

Out to the tall gunslinger's right, a lean man with sinewy legs and a shock of dark hair showing beneath his

11

battered black Stetson — vaguely familiar to Guiana — chuckled softly. The dark, elegant Mexican leaning casually against the poles of the corral with a Winchester dangling half forgotten from his right hand spat into the dust and muttered something under his breath.

'Price?' The tall man shook his head. 'Who the hell mentioned cash changin' hands?'

'I'm a horse trader,' Guiana said, sensing the futility of words, panic rising within him as he thought of Meg, looked for a way out of a desperate situation and found nothing but menace. 'Selling horses is the way I make a living.'

'Living,' the lean man said, 'is something you'd best not discuss,' and the Mexican laughed.

He was still laughing when his Winchester flicked up. A shot blasted, shockingly loud in the dawn stillness. From the house a woman cried out in fear as the bullet clipped Guiana's left heel and took his leg from under him, spun him staggering. The tall man caught him, hard hands under his armpits, swung him bodily around and slammed him against the corral. Guiana's head snapped back against the top pole. He bit his tongue, felt the hot, coppery blood spurt over his chin. The tall man changed his grip, took a bunch of Guiana's shirt front with his left hand, held him stiffarmed against the poles as he half turned away.

'Take 'em,' he told the lean man in the black Stetson. 'Strip the rigs, then cut out three horses. Yours is the big grey, pick out the two next best — and check all three for them Lazy B brands.'

He punctuated his words with a sharp turn and a ferocious right uppercut that grazed the side of Guiana's head and almost ripped off his right ear as instinctively he twisted away. Through the singing in his head, he heard the creek of timber as the corral was opened, heard light footsteps pattering across the yard, in desperation, drove his knee up hard at the gunman's crotch and felt it hit hard thigh muscle and slide away as the tall man laughed harshly. Then the right fist hit him three times in the face in swift succession, short, pounding blows that loosened teeth, split his eyebrow, turned his knees to water and, but for the iron grip of the man's left hand, would have sent him down.

'Stop it, all of you right now!'

The words were shrill, the voice close to hysteria. An oily double click brought the tall man's head twisting around. Over his shoulder, through blurred eyes, Guiana saw Meg, bulky and awkward in the shift dress straining tight across her belly. The shotgun was at her shoulder. Her face was grim and white as bone.

'You hear me? Let him go or I'll . . . I'll . . . '

But even as she spoke, as the shotgun wavered, as her voice trailed away brokenly, the Mexican was moving like a snake striking. The Winchester came up and around. It cracked against Guiana's chin. The sharp foresight raked his cheek. The muzzle bored into the soft hollow under his torn, bloody left ear.

And all the while there was the sound of the stocky man working in the corral, the whirr of his lass rope, the excited snorting of horses, the dry, throat-smarting taste of the stirred-up dust.

'You pull those triggers,' the Mexican said, 'your man is dead.'

'But you'll die too.'

The Mexican grinned, his teeth flashing white under a drooping mous-tache. He shrugged, said with mock courtesy, 'All right, I let you shoot first. Then you watch me fall down. But what use is that? Your man will have a hole in his head, his brains in the next county . . .'

Meg moaned.

Guiana said, 'Go back to the house, Meg, let 'em take the horses, leave us alone — '

15

The hard fist rocked him backwards. The Mexican leaned on the Winchester, holding it tight against Guiana's neck. And now the tall man with the soft voice and the hard, gloved fist began systematically to beat Guiana, the iron left arm holding him upright against the corral while the right fist sank into his belly, slammed into his ribs, rocked his head back on his shoulders, sent blood flying in a fine spray of bright red droplets that formed a glistening pattern on the peeled poles.

The high ringing in Guiana's ears was distant now, and fading, and over and above it, insistently, unendingly, there was the dull, meaty smack of the vicious blows the man was slamming into his body and head. He was faintly aware of Meg sobbing, of the Winchester's muzzle grinding into the bone behind his ear; of legs as weak as those of a sickly, hour-old fawn.

Then, abruptly, the Mexican moved away. The hand holding his bunched shirt let go and the tall man stepped back. Like a one-legged man whose crutch has been kicked away, Guiana toppled sideways. He slid along the corral's poles, stretched his length in the dust, rolled onto his back with an arm flopping loose. The rising sun poured blinding light into his staring eyes. Voices were jumbles of words, coming to him in waves. Then they faded, to be replaced by the creak of leather, the jingle of metal bits, a hard, rhythmic pounding. The ground trembled beneath his limp body.

And then there was a sudden rush of feet, a soft murmuring, and as gentle arms lifted his head and shoulders and warm tears dampened his face he strained upwards, shook his head to clear his vision, and stared across the yard as the three riders hammered down the slope until there was nothing left but the dust of their passing.

2

'They must have known you, hated you, in the past,' she said. 'Why else would they do that?'

'If you're right,' he said, 'and they caught up with me after what has to be more than five years spent huntin' me down, d'you think they'd leave me alive?'

'Maybe all they wanted to do was teach you a lesson. And they surely did that — didn't they?' She looked at him, the damp, red-stained cloth poised, her eyes troubled, bewildered.

Guiana hitched himself up in the big chair, wincing as pain knifed across his ribs. 'For a lesson to be worth the teaching, the man gettin' taught needs to know the reason behind it. Ain't no use in someone ridin' in out of nowhere and whalin' the tar out of a man unless the feller knows exactly why he's takin' a pounding.'

'But if you know them — '

'Meg,' Guiana said softly, 'that wrangler was familiar enough to nudge a nerve, but I know I never saw those fellers before today. They didn't call me by name. There was no recognition in their eyes. They rode in wantin' fresh mounts — '

'No.' She shook her head fiercely, splashed the cloth in the steaming bowl, squeezed it then leaned forward with difficulty to tilt his head with cool fingertips and gently wipe the caked blood from his torn ear. 'I was scared out of my wits, John, but not too scared to see what was goin' on around me. They rode in on fresh horses, unbranded so they can't be traced, nary a streak of lather on them when that wrangler off-saddled.' She bit her lip, frowning, said distractedly, 'If he was familiar that's because, looked at in a hurry, he could be mistaken for you — and this ear needs stitching, John.'

'Soon's I get to town.'

He reached over and took the cloth from her hand, eased himself out of the chair, his lips tight.

'That's the direction those . . . those men took. I feel sure they were making for Cash's Crossing.' Her eyes were troubled. 'Another possibility is they were small ranchers making a mistake.'

'Mistake?'

'Oh, John, you know there're rumours of trouble. Some big rancher getting high handed. Squeezing smaller spreads too hard. Taking payments for services he forces on them, protection on the big drives for a percentage at the railhead. There was even a talk of bringing a federal man in . . . '

Standing stiffly, Guiana nodded. 'One reason why I raise horses, not cows. But I think you've got this one wrong. Ain't a man out there could take this spread for a big ranch, by mistake. No, there was cold calculation in what they were doing. This was no mistake, Meg.'

20

'All right. But d'you reckon Grit Harding'll listen?'

'He's marshal. A bunch of hardcases just rode in and stole three of my best horses.'

'Or traded.' Meg lifted the bowl, bloody water slopping over the edge as she took a heavy step towards the kitchen. 'Isn't that what they'll say, if he even bothers to go after them?' She hesitated a moment, then added, 'Maybe you'd be better off talking to Liam Brannigan — I've got a feeling you'll be needing someone who's firmly on your side, no matter what . . .'

As he limped across the room and out into bright sunshine, Guiana knew that his wife had made a valid point. He was often of the opinion that in certain important ways she was more wise and experienced than he could ever hope to be, and guessed that the problem had its roots in his previous lawless existence. A man who spends close on twenty years mixing with a bunch of misfits — a man who is himself on the outside of society — is likely to get a one-sided view of life. Figuring out which bank to rob, or how to outsmart a posse is no way to prepare for a married life that began when he was past forty, a frugal living scraped out from horse trading.

He splashed cold water into the tin bowl, remembering how Meg had emerged from the lights and the raucous laughter and the smoke-filled atmosphere of Tombstone's Oriental saloon, a painted saloon girl reaching out to stay the hand that was drifting towards his .45 as he faced up to Wyatt Earp.

Without doubt she had saved his life then. White-faced from the shock of what might have been, he had taken her from the shabby glitter of the Oriental saloon, lost himself in the pure soft velvet of her brown eyes and the next day they had married. A year later, his vow to change his ways still unbroken, he had topped the rise overlooking this Texas valley and it seemed that all of life was sweet with no end to it in sight.

Angrily, he stripped off his shirt and splashed water over his bruised face and upper body. The sun was barely clear of the hills yet he was washing for the second time, the pain now far worse than the biting shock of cold water and the burn of a blunt, open razor. Blood stained the clear spring water. He straightened to towel himself dry, his eyes drifting towards the corral.

That grey was a fine horse. His lips tightened. He took a breath through flared nostrils, tossing aside the damp towel with a gesture that spoke of his anger.

Meg was right. Marshal Grit Harding was unlikely to raise a sweat chasing horses stolen from a reformed outlaw. If he did, that trio of *mal hombres* would lie in his face. But if Meg had got it right, then this bad business had once been Guiana's line of work, not hers. As a saloon girl she had seen both sides of life, but he had ridden this trail of treachery and deceit many times, crossed such men as part of his own wicked trade.

If Grit Harding held back, there was only one course he could take if he was not to be an easy mark for the riders who passed in the night. To ride that trail he would need more than bare fists and the fierce desire to recover what was rightfully his, and it was with a grim, set face that John Guiana turned back into the sun-splashed shadows of his home and opened the old tin trunk.

★　★　★

The ride into town was a painful experience for Johnny Guiana's bruised and battered frame, undertaken on a young and half-broken pony that was smart enough to sense the tension winding his rider up as tight as a spring, mean enough to try to unseat him at least once every mile.

But horses were the outlaw John Guiana's adopted trade. Each time the bronc sunfished, twisted or end-swapped the violent motion of the sinewy frame was met by the rider with absent-minded, practised ease. Dust erupted from beneath the slashing hooves to enfold the battling duo in choking clouds. Then, as the pony reacted to the fierce bite of a curb bit on tight reins and the contest was over until the next spell of action, the dust settled in their wake and the bowed but undefeated pony's frisky canter took them swiftly along the upper reaches of the Nueces towards the town of Cash's Crossing.

On the way — and between bouts of action — Guiana had time to muse on the morning's happenings, but when he was close enough to see the sun washing the flimsy false fronts of the buildings sprawled along the wide, sloping banks of the river and his last cigarette was flicked away, he was still no closer to an answer.

Maybe, he thought, Grit Harding would enlighten him — for if anyone should know of a roving band of horse-thieves moving onto the Nueces, it was the town marshal. Yet even as he urged the pony off the lush grass alongside the river and turned into the dusty main street of Cash's Crossing, Meg's parting words went with him like a haunting echo.

'*Two years since you mended your ways is too short a time, John. In the eyes of Grit Harding you're still no better than the men who stole our horses. My advice would be to let this trouble lie, lick your wounds and spend your anger riding into the hills after more wild stock. And just remember this, John Guiana: after I stepped in to help you walk away from that confrontation with Wyatt Earp, you told me then you would always heed my words.*'

Well, maybe. But dragging a reckless man away from certain death was a mite different from preventing him from recovering property that he had not only paid for in sweat and blood but which, if sold, would go part way to seeing them through the next winter without going hungry.

And if Marshal Grit Harding held him in such contempt that he wouldn't stir from his office, well, it shouldn't take a man long, however rusty he was at his former trade, to pick up the trail of three outlaws riding horses freshly branded with a Lazy B.

Grit Harding had his office and jail at the western end of the town of Cash's Crossing, established thirty years back by an Eastern adventurer keen for solitude who travelled West with high hopes but little money and ran out of cash and energy on the upper reaches of the Nueces. He built his soddy on the east bank, sat outside smoking his pipe in the warm yellow light of the long evenings while men with tangled beards arrived in wagons seemingly packed with women and children and, in the blink of an eye, become his neighbours — and quickly decided that the west bank was, after all, the place he wanted to be.

But human gregariousness decreed that his search for solitude was the quest of a misguided man. Soddies and tar-paper shacks sprang up on both banks of the Nueces. Businessmen moved in to build saloons and gun-smiths' premises and greasy cafés and mercantiles, and a lady of impressive bulk opened a house called Nellie's on the far side of town over the front door of which she hung a red lantern. Her granddaughter still ran the establishment with considerable flair. But while the town adopted Amos Cash's name with much the same wry humour that Johnny Guiana had felt when he called his spread the Lazy B, the Eastern adventurer with a desire for his own company ended up with that, and nothing more, in a log cabin built in the shadow of a low wooded hill some way west of the town that long after his death was still known as Cash's Folly.

★　★　★

Somehow, that word folly refused to leave John Guiana's mind as he rode towards the marshal's office. The ride along the main street was one ride he'd made many times, but today seemed different in a way that was strangely ominous. There was something wrong with the town, and its people. The morning air was electric with tension. He would have expected to see Joe Gates, the big young swamper, washing down the plank-walk outside the saloon and cursing every wagon that trundled by pulling its cloud of dust. He would have expected to see Wink Martin watching Gates with amusement from the doorway of his mercantile as he awaited the first customer; Lee Ryder and his cronies, lounging against the peeling walls of Annie Lawrence's café, bleary-eyed and unshaven after a night's carousing.

But there were no wagons, and the door of the mercantile was closed. The burly, aproned figure of Wink Martin was fifty yards down the street, the centre of a huddle of figures outside Mig Angelo's livery barn. And instead of waiting with a rumbling belly outside Annie's grease joint, the tall, moustachioed figure of Lee Ryder was talking animatedly to Curtis Long outside Morgan's saloon, and as Guiana rode by their glances flicked towards him and he saw eyes widen, Ryder's mouth gape in obvious disbelief.

So it was with considerable puzzlement that Guiana slid gratefully from the back of the wiry bronc, frowned a little as he sniffed the air, loose-hitched the reins to the tie rail and stomped across the plank-walk and into the office of Marshal Grit Harding.

Shadows crossed by slanting sunlight in which dust motes floated fooled his eyes into believing the small room was empty. Then a coffee pot rattled, the aroma of strong java assailed his nostrils, and over at the black, pot-bellied stove a stocky man straightened, turned. Steam misted the air above the tin cup held in his left hand, curling towards his dark, unshaven face. As he moved away from the stove the shiny new '73 Peacemaker .45 knocked against the desk. He lifted the cup, gingerly sipped the scalding liquid, and pinned Guiana with eyes of a chilling shade of ice-blue.

'I'm reporting a theft,' Guiana said. 'Men rode in, stole three of my horses, headed this way.'

'Just like that.' The cold blue eyes swept up and down, taking in the ugly cuts and bruises on Guiana's face, the dark congealed blood on his torn ear, the six-gun sitting uncomfortably in the dried-out leather holster hanging from a stiff belt. 'And why would they do that, Mr Guiana?'

In the silence, Guiana could hear his own shallow breathing, the liquid smacking of the marshal's wet lips against the tin cup, the distant buzzing of a fly. He said, 'They don't need a reason. If you want one, I'd say horse thieves steal because that's their business. They make money by selling horses they don't own. Today it's mine.'

'No men leading horses have rode through the Crossing.'

The words were flat, but now there was an expectancy in the marshal's eyes, an angry flicker of cold flame.

'They left theirs, rode mine,' Guiana said. He swallowed, watching the flare of the marshal's nostrils as, without looking, he placed the cup on the desk.

'Theirs wrung out?'

'Not so's you'd notice.'

'So why trade?'

'Not trade: steal.'

'So they rode in, took your horses, left their own good mounts in exchange?' The blue eyes, now burning with an inner fury, bored into Guiana. 'You make this story up while you washed off the blood from those wounds you got from Wade Fuller's murdered teller?'

'I don't know what you're talking about, but a murdered teller's your business; horse trading's mine, and I can't operate if thieves are allowed to ride off with good stock.'

Even as he was speaking Guiana could feel his stomach muscles tightening. The marshal's words seemed to make no sense, not even as a cynical joke, but while his mind registered the thought it recalled the way he had climbed down off his horse and sniffed the air. He now knew that he had smelt gunsmoke, and he began worrying about that, not sure which way the conversation was leading, sensing trouble.

Grit Harding leaned forward to place his hands flat on the desk, rocking his weight back and forth over his stiff arms. And all the while his eyes stayed on Guiana; cold, calculating.

'Let me tell you about the bank robbery, Guiana,' he said, and there was indifference in his tone, the weariness of a man setting about an unnecessary chore. 'Three men rode in — but, hell, you know that — piled off their horses and walked into Wade Fuller's bank. The only man there — this was right early, if you recall — was Ben Carter. Ben's a skinny feller, but what he lacks in bulk he makes up for in heart. A gun pointin' at his belt buckle don't faze Ben, not when there's a whole town's cash at stake. So he wades in, settin' about one of them cowardly bank robbers with a metal cash box he picks up off the counter, then with his bare knuckles.'

Harding's knuckle joints crackled as he eased back, straightened, flexed his fingers.

'Didn't do him no good,' he said softly. 'Because round about then, with blood pourin' from the ear Ben damn near tore off — '

'What the hell — '

' — with blood runnin' down your neck and drippin' on the floor of Wade Fuller's bank, you pulled that six-gun and you shot Ben Carter dead.'

The words trailed away into a heavy silence.

'You're crazy,' Guiana said hoarsely.

'Three men. Horses bearin' the Lazy

B brand. One of them that big grey you ride.'

'Stolen. Every damn one.'

'No sir.' Harding shook his head emphatically.

'Would I ride into town to rob a bank using horses wearing my brand?'

'One way or another, you'd do it,' Harding said, eyes glittering. 'Like the others, your face was masked by a bandanna, but Deputy Slim Callan was out there and him and half-a-dozen men recognized you. Lean, sinewy, black Stetson, ridin' a Lazy B horse. A grown man don't change his ways; once an owlhoot . . . '

Even as he spoke, his hand was moving. With lazy speed and a bare whisper of sound, Grit Harding smoothly drew his Peacemaker and thumbed back the hammer.

'So the situation we've got is this, Guiana,' he said. 'You turn around and walk out of here, I shoot you in the back, and within my rights a-doin' it. You figure stayin' put's a better option,

I'll lock you in one of them cells back there. That happens, you've got my word: the next time you see the light of day'll be when you walk out into the cold dawn, and when you do that you'll be maybe thirty short strides away from gettin' your neck stretched for bank robbery and murder.'

3

The six-gun clattered across the office. The impact of the fall dropped the hammer. The explosion sounded like a charge of dynamite going off, and the wild slug shattered the dusty window with a tinkle of falling glass. At the same time, the coffee cup hit the wall with a metallic clank, splashing scalding hot coffee into Grit Harding's face as he skidded backwards over the desk. With a bellow of anger and pain he slid off the far edge. As he hit the floor with the back of his neck, his booted feet kicked over and slammed into the stove. It rocked perilously. Hot embers hissed in the pools of fresh coffee. Harding's bellow turned into a howl of agony. He rolled frantically, pawing at his face.

On the other side of the desk, half listening for the sounds of Deputy Slim

Callan returning, Guiana watched the performance narrow-eyed as he blew onto the bruised knuckles of his right hand. The mighty blow aimed at the angle of the marshal's jaw had connected with the power of a swung fence pole. The action had been instinctive, compounded of fury at Harding's words and the weight of frustration that had been building inside him ever since the earlier beating.

The marshal had offered him two unattractive options; Guiana had chosen a third that was as satisfying as it was unexpected.

But as Harding's howls of pain subsided to low groans emitted from between clenched teeth, the marshal, recovering fast, came up onto his knees to glare at the horse trader through red, streaming eyes, Guiana knew he was still in deep trouble. Already boots were pounding along the plankwalk, drawing rapidly closer as Lee Ryder and Curtis Long responded to the sudden gunfire. Shouts could be heard ringing out from the opposite direction, and Guiana knew that Wink Martin would be limping across the road from the livery barn accompanied by the fiery Mexican hostler with his battered Sharps carbine. And, on the floor of the office, Grit Harding had recovered his .45 and was thumbing back the hammer as he thrust up off his knees with a growl of fury.

With a movement as instinctive as the looping right hook delivered to the marshal's unprotected jaw, John Guiana's hand dipped to his holster. It was done without conscious thought, an oiled move from stillness to instant action honed by years riding the owlhoot trail when lightning-fast reactions made the difference between riding out of one more border town or leaving in a pine box. He looked coolly into the stocky marshal's blazing blue eyes as he came up off the floor. He saw the lawman's pistol lifting as the butt of his own Colt smacked against his palm and the pistol snicked smoothly out of the stiff leather holster.

And it was up, his thumb levering the hammer as Marshal Grit Harding snarled his fury, when the office door crashed back against the wall. Someone yelled. A mighty blow struck the back of Johnny Guiana's head. There was the sudden taste of copper in his mouth. Then that was gone as he fell forward into a lightning storm that exploded in his brain and carried him upwards and outwards to distant, silent stars that were beyond his reach.

★   ★   ★

He came to with a start, eyes snapping wide as he rolled sideways off the iron cot to hit the dirt floor with a solid thump that sent a bolt of pain shooting through his skull. His right hand scrabbled at his hip, found nothing but empty leather; his mind sought coherent thought, found only confusion hidden behind a dull, throbbing ache.

A slow, ironic hand clap brought him

to a sitting position, elbows on his knees, neck bent so that his right hand could gingerly touch the lump on the back of his head. His fingers found hair matted with dried blood. Pain was a sharp knife piercing his brain and bringing a belly sickness welling acridly into his throat.

'From here,' Liam Brannigan said, 'that looked suspiciously like the fumbling of a worn-out shootist who has trouble figurin' out what day it is, never mind his pistol.'

'Monday,' Guiana said thickly. 'It started well, then turned into a farce.'

With careful concentration he climbed to his feet and walked unsteadily to the strap-steel bars, clung onto them to peer at the tall man who was sitting easy on the bench in the passage.

'Business or pleasure, Liam?'

'You know damn well I give up sin-bustin' ten years ago when ornery varmints like you began outnumberin' honest fellers like me.' He lifted a hand to scratch his thick dark hair, said quietly, 'They say the man who gunned down Ben Carter looked awful like John Guiana — even with a bandanna pulled up over his ugly face.'

'So I ride into town, murder Ben Carter, ride out with a gunny-sack stuffed with bank notes then come back a couple of hours later like nothing had happened?'

'Unlikely, even stupid, but certainly possible.'

'Is that the way you see it?'

'What I see don't carry no weight, John. It was all I could do to stop Lee Ryder and his hangers-on from stringin' up a man who was halfway to dead already.'

'But you did — you, not Grit Harding — and now you're here,' Guiana pointed out, and he poked a hand through the bars as the man who had once been an itinerant preacher came up off the bench to offer matches and his sack of Bull Durham.

His face suddenly serious — his tone

no longer joshing — Brannigan said, 'The whole town's rose up against you. Three men rode in, robbed the bank, killed a harmless friend. They figure they've got one of them fellers.' He paused, watched the floating cloud of smoke as Guiana applied a match to his cigarette. 'You know there's no chance you'll ever come up before a judge?'

Guiana pondered, felt his bruised lips react to the bite of the tobacco, tasted the more potent bitterness of despair. 'I feel bad enough without you passin' me more dismal news.'

'Unless we do something, fast, you're a dead man standin' up.'

'What about the Crossing's decent men?' Guiana said. 'Wink Martin will get past his anger, recognize the truth. Mig Angelo don't think too highly of Grit Harding. Billie Morgan runs a saloon, but anyone who's come up against him at five-card draw knows he's got a mind that can cut through most kinds of nonsense.'

Brannigan shook his head. 'What

they're seein' is an ex-owlhoot they exchange the time of day with suddenly reverted to old ways. You come up with something they can get their teeth into, they'll listen. But in eight hours it'll be dark; Lee Ryder'll be drunk enough to howl, and Grit Harding ain't likely to stand in the way of a drunken mob carryin a rope and bayin' for blood.'

'Eight hours. Most of an ordinary day, but the blink of an eye when it marks the time a man has to live.'

Guiana bit off the words, then turned away to contemplate the glowing tip of the cigarette while ruminating with some gloom.

Out at the Lazy B, Meg would be going contentedly about her chores. Ordinarily, the most that would concern her would be for how many more months she could keep wearing her ordinary work clothes, and whether Marshal Grit Harding was being accommodating or pigheaded. But if the news of her husband's arrest reached her, it would be carried from the Crossing by those ready to gloat. Even in her despair, for the wife of an owlhoot gone bad there would be no help.

As he turned to look speculatively through the drifting cigarette smoke at the gangling ex-preacher, Guiana knew that the picture painted by Liam Brannigan was painfully accurate. Reaction to a bank robbery affecting most businessmen in town would be resentment and anger in which there would be no room for mercy. It would take time for common sense to surface — and time was what he was short of.

And that left Liam.

'Is that what you came for — to cheer me up by readin' my sentence of death?'

Brannigan grinned. 'In the yard behind places like this I used to read last rites.'

'And now?'

'Well, right now I need something solid I can take to those sensible folk you mentioned.'

Guiana met the grey, level gaze of the man known as Sky Brannigan, and saw lurking deep in those eyes an emotion that was at odds with the casual, carefree manner that he knew now was feigned; saw there a steely hardness that could be intimidating or reassuring, depending on which side of the fence a man sat.

'Tell them,' he said carefully, 'that three men came to the Lazy B at dawn and stole my horses, then used them to ride in and rob the Cash's Crossing bank. Tell them, if walk I out of this jail, I intend to bring those men to justice.'

Brannigan grunted approval. 'Short, simple, to the point. But whatever you say ain't going to budge the worthy Grit Harding — and in those words there's a clear invitation for someone to come along and bust you out of here.'

'Yeah,' Guiana said huskily. 'And if that falls on deaf ears and they still plan on stringin' me up for something I didn't do, ask them why the hell a man would rob a bank when there's a woman out at the Lazy B carryin' his unborn child.'

Flame flared in the grey eyes. Sky Brannigan nodded.

'Right now, I can't think of any question more likely to change a few minds.'

★ ★ ★

How long must a man wait to know if he will live or die? How long before the anger of decent men cools, before the raw fumes of cheap whiskey dissipate and clear heads direct hardworking hands to toss aside the hang rope in sudden disgust?

For Guiana, four of the eight hours decreed by Sky Brannigan passed in fitful sleep. Four more crawled by in long minutes measured by the inching of a bright shaft of sunlight across the dirt floor of Guiana's hot, airless cell. When that broad beam faded to a fiery lance then winked out as the red orb of the evening sun sank behind the buildings overlooking the rear of the jail, the distant sound of men's raucous voices as they tossed back jolt glasses of false courage in Billie Morgan's saloon took him to the strap-steel bars, saw him with fingers hooked as he hung on and stared with unseeing eyes into the gloom of the passage.

All he could see was the cold surface of a stone wall. All he could hear was the gathering of a lynch mob.

He was fixed in that position when Grit Harding opened the office door and came through in a flood of lamplight with a tin plate of grub, a cup of steaming coffee; placed them on the floor while he drew his six-gun and unlocked the cell door, then nudged the drink and vittles through with the toe of his boot.

No words were spoken. The marshal's unshaven face glistened with the drying sweat of a long hot day, his body exuded its sour stink. The blue eyes cut cruelly through the lamp-lit gloom, razorsharp knives of cold disdain that stripped Guiana of hope as the door was locked, the heavy bunch of keys jingling and clattering against the metal. The marshal turned and left, slamming the office door. And with teeth clenched and the dead weight of a numbing frustration bearing down on his shoulders, Guiana turned bitterly away to swing a booted foot that sent cup, plate, coffee and hot food flying across the strap-steel cell.

It took another cigarette fashioned from Sky Brannigan's makings to settle his jangling nerves, a half-hour of pacing in taut silence — made the more painful by the soporific night sounds and scents of Cash's Crossing being enjoyed by men who were free — to see the inevitable return of the cold fear pushed only briefly to the back of his mind by Grit Harding's visit.

Fear dragged him to the iron cot, dumped him in a cramped sitting position against the cold wall, wrapped his arms around his drawn-up knees and fixed his eyes on the passage, turned every tiny sound into a palpable threat to his life.

Then that fear became a living, squirming beast that brought the cold sweat springing to his brow and again took him, quivering, into the centre of the cell when voices sounded in the office, suddenly, shockingly loud. A door crashed — open, shut? A hard object that, in Guiana's fevered imagination, became the barrel of a shotgun, banged solidly against the door.

The door swung open.

A tall man stepped through, stood unsteadily, a swaying black shape against the yellow light of the office lamps. Blinking, Guiana saw that the metal that had banged against the door was a tin cup. The slopped coffee threaded a bright trail down the woodwork. Then the man's raw, rich chuckle broke the tense silence and, transfixed in his cell, Guiana swore that each of his muscles creaked as it relaxed, and his involuntary swallow was dry and painful.

'Jesus Christ!' Guiana said.

'No, it ain't,' Deputy Slim Callan said with grave dignity, at the same time canting his angular frame slowly sideways to lean drunkenly against the wall. 'And if it was, goddamn it, even he wouldn't help the bank-robbin' sonofabitch who plugged poor old Ben Carter.'

'If he could find him,' Guiana said. 'Because sure as God made little apples, he ain't in this cell.'

'Hah!' Blinking owlishly, Callan rattled the cup against his teeth as he drank, took it away to wipe the dregs from his straggling moustache and whiskery chin with his sleeve, then wobbled away from the wall on boots with badly run-over heels to come close to the bars and glare at Guiana.

'Grit Harding reckons he's here,' he said with belligerence. 'Wade Fuller reckons he is, Billie Morgan reckons he is; Mig — '

'For Christ's sake, Slim, cut it out!' Guiana said fiercely. 'Get a hold of yourself, then go get those keys off the hook out there and open this cell before it's too late.'

'Keys?' Slim Callan said, drawing himself up and frowning then attempting to turn his head as, behind him, something musically jingled. But the effort was too much of a strain on his alcohol-soaked equilibrium. A step to catch his balance found his long legs tangled, this time he toppled against the bars like a sapling lopped off at ground level — and, as he leant there puzzling over Guiana's last words and gradually wilting, Sky Brannigan slipped through the door like a wraith and in two long strides had the muzzle of a six-gun jammed hard under the gangling deputy's lantern jaw.

4

'Goddamn!'

Sharpe Eagan, the tall man with the swarthy face of an Indian and leather gloves stiffened with the blood of John Guiana, swore softly into the darkness behind Mig Angelo's livery stable.

Watching him, the Mexican hostler shrugged expansively. 'It is true. The others will stand back from a lynching but, with Harding elsewhere, Brannigan will do more: he will walk into the jail and bring out John Guiana.'

'What about the deppity?' Con Shipley, the wiry man with the dark hair and black Stetson whose face now showed the marks of Ben Carter's violent resistance, was down on his haunches against the wall, idly using a finger to draw in the dust.

'Drunk,' Angelo said. 'In any case

he'd listen to Brannigan's silver tongue, do as he asks.'

'Then we rob again, elsewhere, pin it on Guiana, get him wanted by every lawman in Texas.'

This was the Mexican, Tony Cruz, Winchester in one hand and a black cheroot smouldering in the other. In the heavy silence he let the words wash over the other men, then stepped out of the stable's runway and chuckled. 'Hell, it's too easy,' he insisted. 'Lettin' that feller over at the bank cut you up a little was a lucky break, Con. Right now, you and Guiana are like identical twins got caught in a stampede.'

As the battered wrangler snorted his disgust, Eagan said, 'Yeah, but we've got them three Lazy B mounts, and Mig's holdin' that wild bronc Guiana rode in, under strict orders from Harding.'

'Harding's working with us, so releasin' the bronc won't be a problem once he knows what's cookin'.'

'There is another, better way,' Angelo

said. 'Guiana is already a bank robber and a murderer. Soon, with the benefit of my generosity, he could be a horse thief.'

'You're not thinkin' straight,' the wrangler objected. 'For this to work we need two horses look the same.'

'I have two blood bays,' Mig Angelo said, his teeth flashing white. 'A matched pair, tough cow ponies, the kind of horse a man on the run would kill for — or steal.'

Con Shipley grinned. 'One for me, one for him.'

'Who the hell'd work that one out, or believe it iffen they did?' said Tony Cruz with grudging approval.

'With that settled,' said the tall man, 'all we need's another bank.'

'Youngstown spends most of its time sleepin',' Shipley said.

'Also, it is on the way home,' said Tony Cruz, the Mexican.

'And from them timid Mormons I ain't likely to get a second beating,' said the wrangler.

The tall man slammed a gloved fist decisively into his palm. 'Go get that blood bay, Mig. John Guiana and his owlhoot cronies're about to rob another bank.'

5

'Stay nice and still,' Liam Brannigan ordered, as, with his free hand, he inserted a big key in the lock and twisted. The stiff lock clicked. With a thin squeal, the cell door swung open.

'Over to the cot with him.'

Together, his loose arms flopping over their shoulders, Guiana and Brannigan manhandled the drooping deputy into the cell and dumped him on the cot. He hit hard, rolled onto his back and at once began snoring. His wispy moustache fluttered with each damp, whiskey-larded exhalation.

'He'll do,' said Brannigan, straightening with a grunt.

'I guess Harding went off to his room in the hotel — but what about the others?'

The tall man grinned without mirth.

'Harding's hanging around somewheres, like a bad smell — or maybe across the river knockin' on a door lit by a red lamp. The others agreed to hold off, forget the lynching — but that's all.'

'No help?'

'For what you done they'll see your neck stretched — but done legal. So they're lookin' to Grit Harding keepin' you locked up until the circuit judge hits town.'

Guiana grunted. 'What you're doin' won't make them too happy.'

By now they were out of the cell, the door securely locked on the snoring deputy, the bunch of keys tossed carelessly onto his chest. Carefully, Guiana eased the office door open, let light flood through, squinted towards the dusty windows beyond which Cash's Crossing's main street was a wasteland of lamp-cast shadows.

Sky Brannigan touched his shoulder.

'Not that way.'

'I left my horse hitched — '

'Been moved to the livery barn.'

'Mig?'

Brannigan's eyes glinted. 'Always was a maverick, and I always figured if he took sides in anything he'd choose the one that gained him the most. But his ma had the gift of second-sight — so they say — and if Mig inherited a tenth of that alongside his horse sense he'll see with more clarity than those stubborn cusses who're aimin' to see you strung up.'

The jail's back door was rarely opened. Rusted bolts took muscle and strong fingers to move, screeching in protest. Cool air drifted in as the door grated open. Guiana pulled a face at the stench of dumped garbage, then stepped out into the back alley and flexed his shoulders.

'Damn! My gunbelt's on a hook in the office.'

'Was.'

Despite the gravity of the situation, John Guiana chuckled at the veteran sin-buster's laconic reply, and the sheer gall of the man. 'That old pistol of mine,' he said softly, 'has had more use in one day than it's had in the past two years.'

'And more to come,' Brannigan said soberly.

Metal glinted. Leather whispered, as Brannigan unbuckled and handed over the stiff gunbelt. With the belt about his waist again and the old, familiar weight snug against his right thigh, Guiana felt a warm flood of confidence. He waited until Brannigan had eased the door shut, then turned and led the way along the alley, moving beneath the unlit back windows of the buildings as silently as the mounds of litter would allow.

Every twenty yards or so, the light from the street's oil lamps washed down the narrow alleys cutting between the various business premises. Once, a man drifted past the far opening, and Guiana tensed as he caught the twin glints of moonlight under the brim of the Stetson that denoted a swift glance, melted into the deep shadows against a mouldering timber wall as the man turned to start into the alley. Then he stopped. A match flared in cupped hands. Smoke drifted across the lamplight as the flame died, and the man went on his way taking with him the faint pinprick of light that was his freshly lit cigar.

Then they had reached the alley whose opening lay directly across the street from the livery barn.

'From here's the only tricky stretch,' Sky Brannigan said behind him. 'Runnin'd feel good, but look bad, won't get you nowhere but back in jail. Best you can do is walk nice and slow, hope there ain't nobody out there knows you by sight.'

'My problem,' Guiana acknowledged. 'I thank you now for all you've done, but this is where we part company. You're already in deep trouble . . . '

Brannigan gripped his shoulder with steely fingers, chuckled low and soft. 'Slim Callan's soaked up so much liquor he won't remember a damn thing about you or me. Far as Wink

61

Martin knows, I was headed home. So as well as the worry of a bank robbery, the town's now stuck with a ghost who lets prisoners out of jail.'

An encouraging push in the back from a firm hand started Guiana into the intersecting alley. A cold waft of air on his back told him that the sinbuster had faded into the night. Without turning, he hitched his gunbelt and strode towards the street lights, hugging the wall. A tin can rolled, clanking. Somewhere, out of sight, a man laughed.

Then he had reached the street and, without pause but slowing his pace to a feigned nonchalance, he set off at an angle across the wagon ruts towards the welcoming shadows beyond the massive, open doors of Mig Angelo's livery stables. He was conscious of an unbearable stiffness in his limbs, of sound and movement everywhere, of lights and laughter and the tinkling of a piano from Billie Morgan's saloon, and of a horse being ridden at a walk down the centre of the street.

But he was shocked when someone spoke, close by, a question in the voice. Instinctively, Guiana mumbled something he hoped sounded like 'goodnight', keeping his head ducked and half turned to the blind side.

Suddenly he was across, and approaching the big double doors. In that instant of realization relief was so strong it was like the first ice-cold drink washing down a throat parched by sun and dust, the first drawn breath taken in warming spring sunshine after a winter spent snowed in. His eyes narrowed to peer down the gloomy runway. His nostrils twitched at the warm smell of horses and the drier, dustier scent of crisp, fresh hay. He was inside. The myriad sounds of night life in the Crossing faded into the background, taking with them the overpowering sense of menace.

And in the sudden soft silence that enveloped John Guiana in its comfortable, reassuring embrace, a hard hand reached out of the darkness to clamp its fierce grip on his shoulder.

6

Saddle leather creaked. The conchos on Mig Angelo's black sombrero winked in the moonlight. The wiry blood bay nickered softly, then settled as Johnny Guiana reached down to pass a soothing hand over its muzzle.

'Maybe tomorrow,' Angelo said gloomily, 'you will find a posse hard on your heels.'

'We'll play cat and mouse along the river and up into the hills to the east,' Guiana said, 'but one way or another I'll give them the slip and find the men who stole my horses and gunned down Ben Carter.'

'Better the other direction,' Angelo said, frowning. 'You head west, there will be open space, room to manoeuvre. Also, big ranchers over that way don't listen to rumours. Hard-headed, they have a contempt for crooked lawmen, will maybe help you.'

'Yeah, but what I need right now is solitude,' Guiana said. 'I need time to think this through, Mig.'

The close-sewn conchos on the sombrero jingled faintly as Angelo bobbed his head. 'I know now I was wrong believing you were involved, but if I had been asked at the time to swear on the Bible, I would have done so . . .'

'Blood runs hot,' Guiana agreed, 'when pistols are a-poppin'. But in the dawn light I saw a man matching my build when his pard was whalin' the tar out of me. I'm not sayin' they planned it that way but, along with the Lazy B brand on those horses, to have a feller riding with them looking like me was damning.'

'But now you are out of jail, and running.'

'By the skin of my teeth. The last thing I expected was to run into Grit Harding.'

'He wanted to look at that half-wild

bronc you rode in.' Angelo's teeth flashed white in a dazzling grin. 'I saw you come out of the alley and start across the street, left that *mal hombre* to nose around that horse he thinks maybe will end up as his.'

'Is that all he came after?'

'Sure.' Angelo shrugged expansively. 'What else, John?'

'I don't know. It's just . . . anyway, the fact is you saw me comin' and grabbed me before I barged in and got my fool head shot off.' Guiana nodded, reached down from the saddle to grip the hostler's hand. 'It carries on this way I'll be owin' debts I can't repay to more men than I can count.'

'It is nothing. If it was of help, I would also have given you my singleshot Sharpes,' and he acknowledged Guiana's lifted eyebrows with a brilliant, flashing grin. 'Now, go quickly — and *vaya con Dios, amigo.*'

'*Hasta la vista*, Mig,' Guiana said, and, with a wry grin of appreciation, he nudged the blood bay with his heels

66

and moved it along the alley behind the livery stables.

Just ten minutes had passed since the hard hand of the little Mexican had gripped his shoulder, stopping him in his tracks. At Angelo's bidding he had moved like a shadow past the office to an empty stall, the murmur of voices like the whisper of distant bird's wings as the hostler engaged Grit Harding in conversation and gradually and with infinite patience shepherded the lawman back up the runway to the lamplit street.

It was then, with the marshal making tracks towards Billie Morgan's saloon, that Angelo had suggested to Guiana that the Lazy B brand had been contaminated by the work of thieves and murderers, and it would be wise for him to change mounts. His offer of the wiry blood bay had been accepted and, as he approached the end of the long alley which also brought them to the outskirts of Cash's Crossing, Guiana knew that the horse he was riding would not let him down. Without demur — hell, without even being asked! — Mig Angelo had handed over his finest hunk of horseflesh, the best cow pony Guiana had set eyes on. And as he dwelt for a fleeting moment on what the little Mexican and the tall sin-buster had risked for him, there was in Guiana's throat a lump of profound emotion for which he felt no shame.

But also — and more soberingly — as he pushed the bay along at a fast lick that left the lights of town behind him and saw their yellow glimmer replaced by the waters of the Nueces silvered by the high, floating moon, there came to Guiana the names of those who would ride with the posse predicted by Angelo.

Lee Ryder, for sure, a man who would ride with a posse and shoot a fugitive dead if there were pistols and hard men at his back. Joe Gates, too, for the hulking saloon swamper who carried a ten-year-old brain in the body of a man of thirty would go where

Ryder went, seeing only the bravado that was a flimsy veneer covering the other man's yellow streak.

Curtis Long, forty years old, a stringbean as tough as weathered rawhide? Well, maybe — if he stuck around long enough. Although in one sense a crony of Ryder's, Long was a line rider for Starlight, a sprawling cattle outfit some eighty miles west on the Pecos. Not much was known about him. He had shown up maybe six months ago, been signed on by Starlight's ramrod. When he rode into town it was always on Starlight business, and he rarely stayed more than a day and night. In Guiana's opinion, Long tolerated Lee Ryder, drank with him because the younger man spent most of his life bellying up to Billie Morgan's bar and was hard to avoid, and suffered his company as a price he had to pay on his infrequent visits to town.

It was said, too, that Long hoped some of his own character might rub off on the footloose youngster, though the fact that he accepted this as unlikely maybe explained the flicker of a wry smile that frequently crossed his lean countenance whenever he was with Ryder.

He was a man unlikely to be intimidated by Grit Harding's blustering attempts to raise a posse.

Well clear of town now, feeling safe enough to pull into a stand of cottonwoods and dig once more into Sky Brannigan's pouch of Bull Durham — which was rapidy taking on the sunken shape of a leaking grain sack — Guiana realized he was impressed enough by Long to consider him a useful man to have on his side. What he needed most was someone with a knowledge of the cattle country between the Nueces and Pecos rivers. Outside of Sky Brannigan and Mig Angelo, no man in the Crossing would raise a hand to help him — and word was they didn't come any wiser than the Starlight rider.

But if Long had left town, that would mean following him to his home spread. Which would be no bad thing. Hadn't Mig Angelo already pointed that out? Maybe Starlight was one of the big ranches he'd been talking about — and if he headed west he'd still be clear of the Crossing, the only way he could stay free, and in one piece.

Guiana fired up a quirly, blew smoke with an explosive exhalation that did little to release his pent-up feelings, then eased back in the saddle in the dappled moonlight under the canopy of grey-green leaves.

With those three men out of the way, he concluded, Grit Harding would be scraping around in the dregs of the town, filling his posse with hangers-on with nothing better to do than tag onto the tail of the hardbitten men who would lead the pursuit. A ragged crew making up the numbers that would put the fear of God into fugitives, their only natural-born skills were the ability to stay out of the action when the guns began to blaze, and to ride hard and fast to save their own skins if things went wrong.

Thoughtfully, Guiana spat out a shred of tobacco, flicked away the cigarette and watched it spark away towards the river.

But that danger of his being hunted down — if it existed — was some hours ahead. Slim Callan would sleep the night away. Grit Harding might look in on his deputy before finally heading for his room and his lonely bed — but then again, he might not, and in that case it would be mid-morning before he could raise a posse, a sight longer than that before they got organized enough to pick up his trail.

And if, Guiana mused with a faint smile, he now decided to double back along the river and head straight through the sleeping town in the remaining hours of darkness — as he must do if he wanted to talk to the Starlight rider — then the posse would end up way to the east, blundering about in the heat of the day with no clear idea where he'd headed and with only two men at best with the intelligence to see through his ruse.

So, how many miles had he put behind him since leaving Cash's Crossing? Gazing out over the moonlit terrain, he estimated three, five at most. That distance had taken the wiry blood bay a matter of minutes, its long, raking stride eating up the ground. The return would need to be more circumspect, the eager horse held back and splashing though the waters close to the banks of the Nueces. And for most of that time horse and rider would be in the open, exposed by the light of a moon now floating through clear skies.

But only three men knew he was out and running, and one of those was locked in a cell. Given luck, Guiana decided, he should be clear and riding west from Cash's Crossing within the hour. And that, he figured, would make it not too long after midnight, giving him at worst ten hours' start on a posse, at best a full twelve.

For a moment, as he moved the blood bay out of the cottonwoods and turned its head once more towards town, the tug of the valley that was his home was so strong it tightened his hands on the reins, turned his own eyes northwards. The impulse to head for his home spread threatened to overwhelm him. It crossed his mind that a swift visit to reassure Meg could do no harm, would ease both their minds and put him in better shape for the tough work that lay ahead. But the thought, as fleeting as it was strong, was over-powered by a heavy jolt of common sense: the Lazy B was the first place a posse would go. If he'd been there, however fleetingly, Meg's gentle eyes would gainsay what her lips were telling the wise men on the lead horses, for there was no worse liar in the whole of the West.

Guiana was forced to admit that, subconsciously, he was remembering what she had done for him in the past and the temptation to visit her was a despairing cry for help. But that common sense, when it kicked in, was also telling him that despite what she had done for him in the past, this time it would take more than the impulsive actions of a courageous woman to save his life.

So it was with a wry smile that John Guiana touched the lean horse with his spurs and sent it at an easy trot towards the Nueces, and the risky ride through Cash's Crossing.

* * *

Over the years, the town of Cash's Crossing had sprawled outwards to east and west, but the original buildings — erected when a white-bearded Amos Cash had given up hope of solitude and retired to his folly, and now somewhat dilapidated — pressed close to both banks of the Nueces. Here the deep waters of the river flowed up to eight feet below the level of the land, and in many places it was possible for a man to ride beneath the steep banks with only the bobbing tip of his Stetson to mark his passing.

John Guiana had witnessed this phenomenon several times on his trips to town, most often in the dry heat of mid-summer. Sometimes, when a bunch of skinny kids had been swimming in deep water, one or more of them had breathed in when he should have breathed out and started choking and screaming, and Mig Angelo, or a passing waddy, had grabbed a rope, run down to the river to swing a long loop and pull them to the bank like half-drowned dogies.

Now he was seeing it from the viewpoint of those kids, and as the blood bay splashed along the gravelly shallows there was a deal of comfort to be had from knowing that if anyone out there *was* watching, the moonlight would lose its shine in the soft felt of his black Stetson and he would be no more than a passing shadow.

Nevertheless he was a man on the

run, and under those shelving banks he rode with his eyes straining to look in all directions at the same time so that, by the time he reached the one solid wooden bridge that would force him up out of the river to bypass, he had an almighty crick in his neck and the urge to put spurs to the bay — and to hell with the risk. He didn't give in to the sly voice that was whispering to him to throw caution to the wind, instead enjoying some relief as he eased the bay up the bank, anticipated the rattle of its hooves on the hardpacked earth leading up to the bridge, felt the cool, damp of the river fall behind him so he could breath crisp, clean air.

But even for that small pleasure there was a price to pay.

Over to his left where the main street ran parallel to the river, a piano still tinkled, lanterns still swung gently in the mild breeze painting pools of light, voices could still be heard. Then, above those distant sounds, Guiana heard the drum of hooves on timber, rapidly closing. The horse being ridden across the moonlit bridge nickered shrilly, a wild, spirited sound that was immediately familiar. And caught half on and half off the road, Guiana could either go back or press on — but he could do neither before the horseman was upon him.

His own wild bronc loomed, bearing down. In mid-stream, atop the frisky horse that had scented Guiana from afar and was eagerly anticipating a resumption of hostilities, the burly figure of Grit Harding was leaning forward, reins high in one hand, eyes glinting as he peered ahead at the rider in the black Stetson caught cold across the western end of the bridge.

Recognition was sudden, and disbelieving. A howl of anger rang out. Moonlight flashed as the marshal's hand dipped and came back up holding his Peacemaker. Hooves clattered. The wild bronc screamed in anger as Mexican spur rowels raked its flank.

What happened next was the opposite of what Grit Harding intended, but something John Guiana could have predicted, and watched with joy. Reacting instinctively to the savage bite of the spurs, the wiry pony braced its legs and slid to a halt on the slippery boards. The pause lasted a single heartbeat, the time it took the bronc to coil and explode. When it did it took off from the bridge like a tightly compressed spring that had sprouted four feet. It went up in a deathly silence broken by a sudden squeal and by Grit Harding's shocked yell. The Peacemaker left the marshal's hand as he grabbed the horn. His neck snapped foward as the pony came down to hit the boards hard on four stiff legs. As his Stetson flipped off his head and skimmed towards Guiana, the bronc swapped ends, repeated the manoeuvre so fast Harding's head couldn't keep up — then bucked the marshal clean out of the saddle and over the guard rail to splash with a gargling yell into the deep, cold waters of the Nueces.

7

Dawn was a narrow strip of light spanning the endless eastern horizon, so dazzlingly bright it seared the eyes. Before that awesome brilliance that sent the first waves of warmth licking across the cold land the mists of night shrank back, threadbare white blankets marking the course of the Nueces river and a hundred small creeks, that flattened then withered to a weak transparency before dissipating like gunsmoke in the aftermath of battle.

By comparison, the dust of the posse was a dun-coloured trailing plume whose tail-end soared high behind the pursuing horsemen, thinning to a pale-yellow smudge drifting against the intense light but always rejuvenated as, at its van, the thundering hooves of the horses drove on across the prairie.

Five miles, John Guiana calculated,

tight-lipped, and lowered his field-glasses. Six men, riding hard — but heading in a direction that pointed some way north of his own more southerly route. What they were doing was following a line as straight as an arrow, and to hell with searching for tracks. Harding had decided there was only one place Guiana could be making for if he left the Crossing and headed west, and that was the Mexican border.

Which was halfway to the truth, but took no account of his reasons.

Made clumsy by the stiffness that came from a long night's hard riding, he pushed away from the boulders and jogged back down from the high ridge to where the blood bay was ground-tethered, stowed the glasses in his saddle-bag and swung into the saddle.

When he gently nudged the big bay's flanks and moved off at a fast canter, there was a sour taste in his mouth put there by warm canteen water, a numbing fatigue, and the leaden weight of a despair that had been considerably lightened by his observations of the posse from Cash's Crossing.

His encounter with Grit Harding at the bridge had questioned his tactics and dented his confidence, suggesting as it did that when doubling back through the town he had foolishly ignored obvious risks. Every town sleeps, but among its citizens there are always those who emerge wide-eyed and bushy-tailed when daylight fades in the west and stubbornly refuse to bed down until dawn. Grit Harding had bedded down, Guiana thought wryly but, just as Sky Brannigan had earlier suggested, his bed had been a shared one richly perfumed, and faintly but luridly illuminated by the red lantern that hung over the door of the infamous premises known as Nellie's.

Which had been to Guiana's advantage, he ruefully admitted. A Grit Harding with his mind on his official job and not lingering in the warm embrace of the painted woman he had just left would have stayed aboard the bucking bronc, ruthlessly battered it into submission with the barrel of his Peacemaker then turned the weapon on the man who had escaped from his jail.

And I don't yet know, John Guiana admitted, by how much the sharp edge of my skills has been dulled by time.

But five miles was a comfortable cushion. The chasing posse would overtake him, but some way to the north, and that fitted in with his own plans. In the dark hours before dawn, he had concluded that the eighty miles to Starlight was too far to be covered in a single spell and would run the heart out of the wiry horse. Roughly halfway between the east fork of the Nueces and the Pecos there lay the small settlement known as Youngstown. Renamed, and inhabited now mostly by a relaxed Mormon group who had broken away from Brigham Young's wagon-train and travelled south, Youngstown was sleepy enough for his arrival to go unnoticed and, if Guiana's memories of the town were correct, there was a tonsorial parlour where he could indulge in a hot bath, a rooming-house where he could maybe grab a couple of hours' sleep.

And if he was again foolishly ignoring obvious risks, then to hell with it!

The rising sun was low at his back, the shadow of the sinewy blood bay long and rippling like something living being chased over the ground as Guiana pushed on across the undulating prairie towards Youngstown. A mile, two miles, five miles. The horse's shadow shortened, the sun warmed perceptibly, the terrain gradually became rougher and split by arroyos and dry washes. Inevitably his progress was slowed as he was forced to pick his route, making lengthy detours around impassable sections that sometimes amounted to doubling back and crossing his own tracks in his efforts to find a way through.

Even with the posse some way to his north, Guiana retained his caution. But the deeply scarred landscape restricted his line of sight so that in many places he was riding blind to everything beyond some fifty yards or so. At a point where seeing even that short distance was impossible, he rode around a stand of stunted trees tight up against the wall of a shallow arroyo — and drew rein so fast the bay sat on its haunches.

The rifle pointing at him was rock steady, the rider on the dun pony standing favouring a foreleg relaxed, nonchalant almost to the point of indifference. He turned his head and spat, said quietly, 'One slug now would line my pockets with gold. Before I left the Crossing, word was the price on your head was a thousand dollars.'

'Easy come, easy go,' Guiana said. 'You'd lose it when it came to light you'd shot the wrong man.'

'Yeah, but with that much *dinero*,' Curtis Long said wistfully, 'it'd surely be worth my while to cross the border at Langtry and take to wearin' a *serape* and one of them big, fancy sombreros.'

'A six-foot, blue-eyed Mexican?'

Guiana said, and Long laughed with genuine humour, tilted the Winchester and slid it into its boot with a soft thunk.

'My horse threw a shoe. Made ridin' such a slow process I heard you some ways back.'

Guiana nodded, nudged the bay forward. 'There's a blacksmith at Youngstown, a hostler who'll fix you up with a horse if that foreleg's too bad.'

'Is that the way it was with you?' Long asked softly, and his eyes flicked pointedly to the rangy blood bay. 'A cow pony like that's worth a heap, turn on a dime, hold still on a taut rope . . . so, did you figure, what the hell, rob the bank, gun down a cashier, steal a fast horse from that no good Mex?'

'You think the same as the rest of them?'

Long eased the lame dun pony round in a tight turn, leaned down to watch the animal's leg as he moved off ahead of Guiana. Apparently satisfied, he straightened, waited until Guiana was

86

alongside and said, 'Whether I do or I don't shouldn't bother you. I put up the rifle, which tells you all you need to know.' He looked hard at Guiana. 'Let's just say the evidence makes you guilty as hell — but that don't alter the fact that from where I sit, something stinks to high heaven.'

'Grit Harding don't see it that way.'

Long grunted. 'All a lawman is is someone councillors pin a badge on because no one else'll do the job.' He flashed a grin at Guiana. 'No skills, less brain.'

'So is Harding wrong because he's too stupid to see different — or wrong deliberately?'

'Whoa, now! I'm a Starlight rider gettin' asked questions don't concern him. I as much as told you what you've done or ain't done is none of my business. I left town ahead of you, ain't seen you since — if anyone asks — and that's where it ends.'

Guiana reined back the bay as it edged ahead of the lame dun, fished

Brannigan's sack out of his shirt pocket and tossed it to Long. The Starlight rider nodded his thanks, quickly fashioned a cigarette. A match flared, smoke drifted in the sunlight. Long handed back the Bull Durham, squinted at Guiana.

'Did you do it?'

Guiana chuckled. 'Oh, the burning curiosity of an unconcerned man,' he said softly. He shook his head. 'My three horses were stolen, I took a beating and ended up in jail.'

'But you broke out, and now you're on the run.'

'I left town.'

The Starlight rider eyed him quizzically. 'Seems to me that amounts to the same as what I just said — or am I missin' something?'

The question hung in the air as they rode for almost a mile in silence. Through the shimmering heat-haze the buildings of Youngstown danced along the horizon, distance made uncertain but surely, Guiana thought, no more than a couple of miles ahead. But getting there was taking time. Curtis Long was forced to pick his route carefully, guiding the lame dun over easy ground. Guiana was content to follow, his mind busy.

'After what's happened, Cash's Crossing was too hot for me,' he said, eventually breaking the long silence. 'What happened to put me in jail waitin' for the hang rope was done deliberate. To right that wrong there's questions need to be asked. But when a man works twelve, fourteen hours a day, he don't make too many friends, or keep up to date with saloon gossip.'

'You intend sortin' this out — then goin' back?'

A horse whinnied up ahead as they approached the town. A wagon cut across from the north, pulling dust, and somewhere a child squealed.

'Depends where the answer lies,' Guiana said. 'But there's only one man I know might have some answers to those questions — and I'm ridin' alongside him.'

Curtis Long shook his head. 'Like I said, the evidence says you're guilty. The bank robbers rode Lazy B horses. The man shot dead Ben Carter looked like you, took a pounding from the teller — and I guess you know what your face looks like.' Long turned his head to spit, and there was finality in the act. 'I already said something stinks, but either way it don't concern me, and that's the way it stays.'

It was on that sour note that Guiana kicked the bay into a canter and rode into Youngstown.

★ ★ ★

Living closer to the border the people of the town had adopted Mexican customs, and midday saw them already looking forward to siesta. The one, sun-soaked street was almost deserted and, when Curtis Long turned off to rouse the man running the livery stable,

90

John Guiana rode past a closed bank, a mercantile with a bolted door and the blinds pulled, a town marshal's office so dusty it looked as if it hadn't opened since the war with Mexico.

Youngstown, he approved, had the look of a place that suited him just fine.

He dismounted and hitched the bay outside a tonsorial parlour that looked as closed as every other establishment in town, but wasn't. His hammering on the door brought forth a bewhiskered gentleman in a white apron who puffed cigar smoke, took one look at Guiana's trail-stained appearance and gestured him upstairs. There, a woman with hair like a blue-black shadow poured scalding hot water into a tin bathtub and padded out on naked brown feet. Within minutes of arriving in town his dusty clothes were shed and deposited on a spindly chair along with his gunbelt, and he was up to his shoulders in foaming soap suds with the tension flowing out of his body like warm rain off a tin roof.

Lazy sounds drifted to him through the open window as if from another world. Bridles jingled pleasantly. Someone spoke softly, got an answer in the same tones. A footstep sounded. A loose board creaked. Guiana's eyelids drooped. His thoughts went the same way as the tension, flowing with languid somnolence to a place where a pretty young woman sang softly as she went about her chores and her mind was filled with thoughts of the growing child she carried within her, the husband who had ridden to town to right a wrong and would surely —

The door crashed open.

A big man in a hard black hat and dusty frock coat of the same colour swung a shotgun so that its muzzles were two black, empty eye sockets staring unblinking at Guiana. Behind him other men jostled, crowding close to see over his broad shoulders. Faces glistened with sweat. In the shafts of sunlight drawn pistols glinted.

Guiana flicked a glance sideways,

brought a hand out of the water then froze, his arm extended, dripping water. His gunbelt was rolled on the chair, too far away to reach — and the shotgun was unwavering, the man's eyes eager, his forefinger white on the triggers. Resistance would be foolhardy: the thought flashed through Guiana's mind — bringing with it the hysterical impulse to laugh out loud — that if he had been caught with the pistol already in his hand, cocked, his finger on the trigger, he would have made his move and died as naked as the day he was born.

'All right,' the man with the shotgun gritted. 'Horse thief, bank robber, murderer — step out of that tub.'

Guiana complied. With soapy water running down his legs and pooling slickly on the bare boards he again reached out a hand, and stopped.

'All I want,' he said carefully, 'is my clothes.'

'Leave 'em.'

'But — '

'You're goin' out this world the same way you come in — buck naked.'

The words echoed Guiana's thoughts, this time evoking not crazy laughter but the chill of fear.

'You're makin' a mistake.'

'You and your pards made a mistake when you robbed the bank.'

'If we did, that was in Cash's Crossing. You're obliged to hand me over to Marshal Grit Harding to be dealt with by the law.'

'Sure — for the first robbery and killing.' The black-garbed man's eyes glittered. 'But the loot you got there wasn't enough so you rode here, worked the same stunt not a couple of hours ago.'

'No.' Guiana shook his head, numb with shock.

'Move.' The shotgun waggled.

His wet footprints were dark on the dusty boards as he walked to the door. The big man stepped aside. Eyes wide, the men on the short, narrow landing fell back, stumbling down the stairs to burst through the door into the sunlit street, their voices raised as they excitedly cried out the news to a town that had been shocked out of its midday slumber.

'*He's a-comin' out!*'

'Joseph's bringin' out one of them goddamn bank robbers!'

'Hell, fust time I've seed a man hanged buck naked!'

'Somebody go get a rope!'

The voice in the crowd had put a name to the big man in the frock coat, and any faint hope within Guiana withered and died. He had heard tales of Joseph Tonkin, town constable of Youngstown. His sense of fair play was legendary, the justice he meted out to wrongdoers swift and final, and the ruthlessly efficient job done by the bank robbers in setting up John Guiana was more than enough to convince a man of his blinkered principles that the only justice lay at the end of a rope.

The shotgun muzzle rammed into the small of Guiana's back, tight rings of cold steel grinding into his spine, driving him down the stairs. He stepped through the door into heat that burned his skin like the fires of Hell. In the middle of the dusty street someone stooped, straightened, and an arm was drawn back. A hard lump of horse droppings hit Guiana in the face and broke wetly, and as he jerked his head aside and spat, the gathering crowd roared.

'That's enough!'

The babble subsided to a murmur. A pistol blasted at the rear of the mob. Someone tittered.

'Next man does that,' Tonkin growled, 'gets one of these barrels.

'Hell, all we want is to watch the fun — '

'Where're you a-takin' him — ?'

'Watch him, Joseph, that bank robber's so danged wet he'll slip through the rope!'

The shotgun's blast drowning the explosion of coarse laughter was a cannon's roar compared to the pistol shot, the muzzle belching flame and smoke. Several birds fluttered from the roof of the saloon, clipping the false front and soaring high to circle over the town as feathers floated to earth. A hitched horse squealed. The men at the front of the mob stepped backwards hastily, stepping on toes, drawing angry cries of pain that dwindled to mumbles as the shotgun swung lazily.

'Go home. Go about your business. Get a-hold of your kids. This is a hanging, not a free show.'

The crowd broke up, men drifting away singly, in pairs, boots thudding on plankwalks, the saloon's swing doors flapping as if to echo the flight of the startled birds.

As they dispersed, John Guiana saw, across the street outside the saloon, the burly figure of Marshal Grit Harding. He was lounging in the shade with his elbows hooked on the hitch rail alongside his horse, reflected sunlight lending a dull gleam to his badge. Ranged around him, watching hard-eyed and grim-faced, were men

Guiana recognized.

Lee Ryder was there, tall, rangy, his straw-coloured moustache drooping over his mouth, his eyes laughing at Guiana. Joe Gates was wearing his perpetual look of vacancy as he watched the happenings in Youngstown, but the simple swamper was made dangerous by the butt of his pappy's Dragoon pistol poking out of the waistband of his baggy serge pants.

Guiana had been wrong about Curtis Long: though he had said little when they met, the Starlight rider had clearly turned down the offer of a place on the posse or, more likely, had left town before Harding began recruiting. But, as expected, numbers had been made up by calling on the town's loafers, and behind Harding, Ryder and Gates there were two men Guiana recognized, but couldn't name.

Five men, all members of the Cash's Crossing posse that Guiana had last seen through field-glasses, five miles distant and following a course that should have taken them to the north of Youngstown. But when Guiana had them lined up in his lenses there had been six, and as Joseph Tonkin's hard hands and shotgun pushed him towards his horse and his wrists were swiftly lashed behind his naked back and he poked his bare foot into a hot stirrup and climbed awkwardly into the saddle he found himself thinking about that missing man and wondering who he was, and why he had dropped out of the posse.

Then all thoughts flew from his mind like those startled birds that seemed to be forming the pattern of that day's events, for Grit Harding had pushed away from the hitch rail and, with his posse, was advancing across the street to meet the man who came running from the livery stable carrying a coil of rope.

And the last thing John Guiana saw as he turned his head to look back at the town of Youngstown was the stringbean figure of Curtis Long. He was walking away, shaking his head.

8

A naked man wears the helplessness of a child. Along with his clothes and his pistol, the man called Joseph had taken away any hope John Guiana had of hitting back. He was reduced to naked flesh and blood, savagely bound with rawhide, a pallid, sinewy figure on the back of the blood bay that in the heat of the midday sun was carrying him towards the sparse woodland flanking the Texas settlement of Youngstown. The rope that would slowly choke the life from his naked body was looped over Joseph Tonkin's saddlehorn. The only sounds accompanying him on that short ride to his own lynching were the squeak of saddle leather, the snorting of horses, the occasional uncomfortable clearing of a throat made dry by something more potent than the plains' dust.

That something was fear.

Fear was a palpable stink that rode with the posse, but the fear and unease were not within Guiana but in the minds of men about to perpetrate the unspeakable. In some uncanny way the naked man had acquired a dignity that set him apart from the posse members who had, in their turn, taken on the appearance and furtive manner of owlhoots. Men rode unnaturally, their bodies awkward and stiff in the saddle, their shoulders hunched and braced as if each man there was already fearful of violent retribution. Eyes that had become shifty, squinted through the billowing dust at other riders, then slid swiftly away. A bearded Crossing rider attempted to spit from an arid mouth. Lee Ryder had dropped back, preferring the simple companionship of Joe Gates. Another man's eyes glanced by mistake towards John Guiana's nakedness; the unkempt head at once dipped and jerked aside, and the man abruptly spurred his horse to the head of the posse so that Guiana was behind him, and out of sight.

That put him close to Grit Harding, and the man called Joseph Tonkin.

The only men there, Guiana reflected, who showed no fear, no disquiet at the rough justice they were about to administer. And despite his nakedness, despite the waves of raw fear that at last threatened to overwhelm him as the fringe of parched trees drew near, his thinking was crystal clear. He knew that the strength and cohesion of the posse relied on the iron willpower of those two men and, in each of those two men, that power drew sustenance from a different source.

Grit Harding was a bull-headed lawman who made his own rules and enforced them with six-gun and fists. He was liable to explode into violence if crossed, made snap judgements and saw justice in pure black and white. If flimsy evidence suggested a man was guilty of a crime, Harding would probe no deeper, and he was always willing to turn a blind eye when summary Western justice took its course and cut out wasteful calls on the circuit judge.

But even that assessment of the Crossing's marshal was simplistic, for there were currents running deep within any man and Guiana had not ruled out the possibility of Grit Harding in some way being in league with the men who had robbed Wade Fuller's bank.

But what of the man Guiana knew only by hearsay, the big man, Joseph Tonkin?

As they rode out of Youngstown, his dark frock coat had fallen open and Guiana had seen the badge glinting on the big man's vest. So, that much was confirmed: he was the law in this part of the state and, like Harding, ruled with a rod of iron. He had walked into a tonsorial parlour and arrested a man, wanted for murder and robbery in Cash's Crossing, who had ridden into his town and committed an identical crime. Guiana's knowledge of the Mormon religion's views on the treatment of sinners was vague, but he figured he was right in assuming that cold-blooded lynching would be ruled out — yet still he was heading for a hang-rope.

Why?

Maybe, like Harding, Tonkin didn't see any sense in feeding a man three meals a day while waiting for a circuit judge to ride in on his buggy and pronounce the same verdict a whole town had got to first. Maybe the men who for some reason were intent on pinning a list of bloody crimes to Guiana's vest had gone beyond the pale in Youngstown, their cynical violence cutting so deep that even a man with deep religious beliefs was driven to act. Maybe . . .

But then there were no maybes.

Just a group of grim, silent horsemen forming a tight circle at the foot of a rise. A tall tree casting a dark shadow. A rope's end flipped high to curl over a

bough and snake down. Hard hands
accustomed to roping steers now
turned clumsily to the task of fashion-
ing a hangman's noose.

A terrible sinking feeling in the pit of
the stomach for a man who had never
been more alone.

'All right,' Tonkin said, 'let's get it
done.'

Grit Harding kneed his horse close to
Guiana, reached across to slip the
rough noose over his head and jerk it
tight around his neck. A hard palm
came up, patted his cheek once, twice,
the second a blow hard enough to
knock his head sideways. Cold blue
eyes met Guiana's.

'Thirty short strides to a dawn
necktie party is what I said,' Harding
said softly. 'You made it a mite further
and the timing's all wrong, but in the
end none of that makes any damn
difference.'

'Who put you up to it?'

For an instant a veil dropped over the
cold blue eyes. Then Harding shrugged.

'Hell, I guess you earned the right to know even if it is too damn late. It — '

'You two finished jawin'?'

The big Youngstown constable snapped the words and Harding broke off, his jaw tight. The moment was gone, and those remaining for Guiana were fast ticking away. A rider was down off his horse, securing the rope's loose end to the tree's trunk. He did it roughly, hauling in on the slack, and Guiana's head was lifted and tilted painfully as the noose jerked tight behind his torn left ear.

'There's no easy way of doin' this,' Tonkin said, his black eyes flat and expressionless as he fixed them on Guiana. 'But you know why you ended up with a rope around your neck, and I can't see reason for complaint. Two bank robberies, one murder. What you maybe ain't aware of is when you lit out of Youngstown, one of you rode down my eight-year-old grandaughter, broke both her legs.' Anger flared, was instantly crushed as the big man tightened his lips and turned away.

'That's it.' He nodded to Grit Harding. The marshal jerked the reins and backed his horse until he was behind Guiana's bay. His right hand rose high, swinging a rawhide quirt. There was an instant's pause at the height of the swing, as if the Cash's Crossing marshal was savouring what he was about to do, reluctant to see it end. Then, with an explosive grunt, he twisted his broad shoulders and brought his arm down, lashing at the bay's exposed flank with the tough quirt.

It never hit home.

The bullet whined wickedly, brushing Guiana's upper arm with its hot breath before ripping the quirt from Harding's hand. It was followed instantly by the rifle's sharp crack. The slug hit the big knuckle of Harding's trigger finger, ripped across the base of all four fingers and took most of his hand along with the flying quirt. Blood sprayed Joe Gates's shirt and he yelled in horror, kicking his horse around and away from the marshal. One of the loafers making up posse numbers stabbed a hand for his six-gun. Again the rifle cracked, and the burly man went backwards out of the saddle to lie still on a bed of dead leaves.

The second nameless man took one look at Grit Harding bent over in the saddle nursing his ruined hand, then frantically wheeled his horse and kicked it into a fast gallop away from the trees. As Joseph Tonkin roared his anger, Joe Gates and Lee Ryder took off, hightailing from the scene of a hanging they'd hoped would earn them free drinks back in Cash's Crossing and seen degenerate into a bloodbath.

'The rest of you stand still!'

The rope was tight around John Guiana's neck. Lashed behind his back, his hands were swollen with the blood restricted by tight rawhide. He felt the rangy bay quiver between his naked thighs. Easy, boy, he thought, feeling the first stirrings of panic. Easy, now!

And as the horse, startled by the gunfire and the noise, remembered its years of work on round-up and trail-drive and froze to stiff-legged steadiness, Guiana closed his eyes to the pounding of his heart and breathed a prayer of thanks to Mig Angelo for what had turned out to be the gift of life.

When he opened his eyes again, Curtis Long's dun pony was kicking up dust as the Starlight rider rode him down from the rise, his stringbean form canted back in the saddle, Winchester held with butt on thigh and ready for instant action. He circled, came up behind Guiana, leaned across to part the rope with a single slash of a sharp blade. The rope's short end fell, slapping the rivers of cold sweat on Guiana's naked back.

'Thanks,' he croaked.

'Don't I know you?' Tonkin's voice was tight, his anger barely held in check as he glared at Long.

'Just a drifter lookin' for justice,' Long snapped.

'So why break up a group of upright citizens here on that same mission?'

Long was reaching down from the saddle for the bay's trailing reins. He came up holding them, snapped the Winchester level as Tonkin's hand strayed towards his hip only to fall away. He said, 'A man can't be in two places at the same time. I rode into Youngstown with this feller, after he followed me all the way from Cash's Crossing.'

'Jesus!' Grit Harding said through clenched teeth. 'Get me to a doc.'

'I believe the evidence of my eyes.' Tonkin watched Long balefully as he turned the chestnut and began to lead Guiana away from the trees, swinging the rifle to cover their escape. 'A man ridin' that horse rode in with two companions and robbed the bank. Another man with your build and the black eyes of an Injun damn near killed my grandaughter.'

'Same band robbed the Crossing bank.' Grit Harding ripped off his

110

bandanna. His damp, ashen face was twisted with pain as he clumsily wrapped the sweat-stained cloth around his wrecked hand. 'Hell, you was there, Long, saw it for yourself,' he called after the departing riders. 'Guiana used his own horses for that job, stole the bay from Mig Angelo after breakin' out of jail.'

'The bay's a loan from Angelo, the man's a good friend,' Guiana called over his shoulder.

'Yeah?' Harding yelled into the dust-hazed sunlight. 'So why the hell was Angelo sixth man in my posse?'

'Hold tight,' Long said, and Guiana braced himself as the Starlight rider kicked his horse into a fast canter and he was jolted back against the cantle as the bay's head was snapped forward by the taut reins and it followed the dun. They rode like that for a mile, then another, cutting around the stand of parched trees then heading away from the distant buildings of Youngstown in a north-westerly direction, always with their ears attuned for the thunder of men riding in pursuit, always with their backs cringing in anticipation of the single bullet that would cut them from the saddle.

The town was still a smudge visible through the heat-haze when Long swung off his arrow-straight course to draw rein on a low knoll at whose crest a tall tree was a lone sentinel. There he dismounted to cut Guiana free of his rawhide bonds, then turned, unstrapped the bundle tied behind his saddle and tossed Guiana his clothes, and gunbelt.

'I've been feelin' like a feller caught with his pants down in a bawdy house,' Guiana said a few minutes later, 'but now, with clothes and a six-gun at my hip . . .'

But Curtis Long was not listening. On the south side of the knoll he was intently watching a directionless plume of dust. Waving away Guiana's attempts at gratitude he said curtly, 'Let's ride,' and within seconds the two men were back in the saddle and again hammering hard towards the north-west.

'Watch out for the others,' Guiana said once, meaning Ryder and Gates, then set his mind to riding as Long acknowledged the warning with a jerk of his head and pushed on hard.

Around them the land was flat, the distant horizon rippling in the heat. When, after a considerable distance, Guiana twisted around to look behind him, there was no sign of pursuit and he guessed that the dust plume had been Tonkin riding with the injured marshal towards town. Nor was there any sign of Lee Ryder or Joe Gates, and the first thin smile of amusement twisted Guiana's lips as he mentally complimented himself on the accuracy of the previous day's predictions.

But what of Mig Angelo?

When Guiana had spotted them, the posse had been riding a course that would have taken them way to the north of Youngstown. Soon after that they must have veered south, ridden into town when he was reclining in a bathtub of hot, soapy water with his mind dulled by langour and foolish optimism.

Had Angelo remained on the original course. If so, why? Where was he now? And what the hell was all that talk about the bay being stolen?

The thoughts remained to trouble him for a further ten miles, when the grass underfoot changed from wiry buffalo to a softer, lusher green. The land sloped gently. Lines of cottonwoods appeared ahead, and beyond there was the glint of water that Guiana figured was a minor fork of the Pecos, beyond that again the endless plains fading away to become as one with the washed-out blue of the distant skies.

Cooler air brushed his face. The frantic pace slackened. Content, for the present, to leave the decisions to the Starlight rider, Guiana gratefully followed him when he turned to ride into a glade almost encircled by trees, and there slid from the saddle with a faint groan of protest.

Ten minutes later, they were sitting in the shade with their backs to a tree drinking hot coffee alongside a crackling fire over which hung a blackened pot, and it was easy for John Guiana to believe that the troubles that had descended on him at dawn the previous day and hammered him with unremitting ferocity were suddenly far, far away.

But that was an illusion, and he knew it. A man with widespread influence was using it to wreak vengeance for reasons known only to himself and, until Guiana found that man and confronted him — to conciliate or, at worst, to force capitulation by the power of the six-gun — he was a wanted man with a price on his head and that cash reward would attract not only law-abiding posse members, but bounty hunters out combing the West for pickings that were never easy but always high enough to justify any risk.

For a loner, that would be bad

enough, but while John Guiana was a target for every lawman or wild gunslinger with the ability to read the figures on a wanted dodger, a family looking forward to the birth of its first child would continue to suffer the agonies of separation and despair.

9

'When we met up on the way to Youngstown, you told me the evidence burned a guilty brand on my hide, but something stunk to high heaven.' Guiana squinted at the Starlight rider through a veil of cigarette smoke. 'Right now, evidence makes me guilty twice over, so why the rescue?'

Curtis Long was flat on his back in the shade, his head resting on his saddle, his Stetson tilted forward over his eyes. Without bothering to look at Guiana he said, 'Maybe I figure the fellers dancin' around the stake pokin' you with sharp sticks have gone too far. Seems to me they ain't got the sense to see that one bank robbery and murder pointed the finger at you, a second was so doggone suspicious any intelligent lawman would begin lookin' elsewhere.'

'Two lawmen were a split second

away from stretchin' my neck; was that stupidity, or calculated, cold-blooded murder?'

'You've got your sums wrong,' Long said vaguely, tipping back his hat and looking across the dying fire at Guiana. Then, shrugging that puzzling remark to one side he went on, 'I think you're right on one count, but missed out on another. I know Joe Tonkin's reputation — '

'Yeah,' Guiana cut in grudgingly. 'Ruthless, but honest.'

'So he was actin' not out of stupidity, or in cold-blood, but because the rage inside him at what happened to that kid was like a red rag to a bull.'

'A man, with a man's weaknesses,' Guiana acknowledged, thinking of his own unborn child and imagining his reaction in similar circumstances. 'So, what of Harding? I got that right?'

'For the answer to that one, look back over the years, my friend.' Long sat up, yawned, stretched. 'I'd say Grit Harding knows damn well you were nowhere near either bank. That rules out stupidity, points to murder, and begs the question — why? Harding's a mercenary, so that tells you he got paid.'

Guiana nodded. 'Someone, somewhere, sometime . . . '

A match flared as Long fired up a cigarette. His blue eyes were thoughtful. 'It's no secret you rode the owlhoot before settling in the hills north of the Crossing. But I guess that only makes it more difficult. How the hell can a man operatin' outside the law count the number of fellers he's crossed, good or bad?'

'Ain't no way,' Guiana said. 'If every one of them rode after me I'd be trampled to death.' He watched the Starlight rider, said thoughtfully, 'I rode out of the Crossing because after a jail break Harding had every right to shoot me on sight. Reason I chose this direction is because I had you down as a knowledgeable cuss with roots far enough from town to see the truth clearer than most.' He pursed his lips. 'What I didn't expect was you gettin' in so deep that, as from a couple of hours ago, you're wanted by the law for aidin' and abettin' a killer.'

Long nodded, his grin crooked. 'And the only way to convince the law all I was doin' was help an innocent man escape the hang rope is to find them three bank robbers — or the man who's pullin' the strings. The way I see it is, we sink or swim together.'

'A tall man, eyes like an Injun; a Mex, handy with a saddle gun; a feller looked enough like me for Grit Harding to slam me in a strap-steel cell . . . '

Guiana spoke thoughtfully, his mind elsewhere. And because he was gazing into the distance, pondering the imponderable, he failed to note Curtis Long's sudden stillness, the dawn of understanding in the Starlight rider's intelligent blue eyes.

★　★　★

'You sure you and your men were tailin' the right *hombre*?'

Joe Tonkin was leaning back in his creaking swivel chair, thumbs hooked in his vest, his Spanish rowels gouging deep scars in the surface of his desk. His black eyes were ugly. He had been crossed, and bested. But he was also contemplative. Time had washed away his anger, and straight thinking told him the man called Long had a point. Nobody could be in two places at once. And if the man who broke up the necktie party had been in the Crossing, but still felt justified in rescuing John Guiana, well . . .

Across the room, gazing moodily out of the window, Grit Harding was a bulky figure with his right arm in a sling, the sweat caused by the agony of his shattered hand filming his face.

'I slung John Guiana in the hoose-gow. He broke out, headed this way. We picked up his trail, follered him into town.' He swung around, glared defiantly at the Youngstown constable. 'You prepared to argue with that?'

'I was expressin' interest in the bit that came a while before you throwin' him in jail,' Tonkin said. 'Like, seein' three men ride in and rob the bank.'

'For sure. Guiana, and two others. Rode Lazy B horses.'

'Which Guiana reported stolen.' The challenging grin twisted Tonkin's lips, failed to reach the dark eyes. 'I spoke with a couple of your men. When I suggested that was strange behaviour for a man just robbed a bank, they were inclined to agree.'

'The cashier got in a few good licks before takin' a slug. You take a good look at Guiana's face?'

'Yeah, and I hear he's a horse trader, breaks his own broncs. Ain't unusual for such a man to hit the ground face first.'

Harding grunted scornfully. 'Yeah, and before that he rode the owlhoot for close on twenty years. You got all the answers, tell me how come he rides to Youngstown, and right then the bank gets robbed? You figure someone'd go to all that trouble two times just to frame a no-good who rode the owlhoot for nigh on twenty years?'

'You know,' Joseph Tonkin said, 'that very thought did occur to me — but for the life of me I can't figure out why they'd do that.'

Something flickered in Grit Harding's eyes. His mouth opened, snapped shut. Abruptly, he turned back to the window. Down the street, out of the last rays of the setting sun, two men were riding into town. The marshal stiffened, recognizing Sharpe Eagan and the Mexican, Tony Cruz.

'Goddamn,' he said softly. He licked his lips, turned to see Joe Tonkin watching him, and said quickly, 'You can't figure it because it ain't happenin'. John Guiana's guilty as hell, and no broken hand's gonna stop me pullin' him in.'

'You seem a mite put out,' Tonkin said, one eyebrow raised. 'Was that riders I heard?'

'Cowpokes,' Harding said, and grinned mirthlessly. 'Maybe you could raise your own posse, Tonkin, go chase those phantom riders robbed your bank.'

'I just might do that, Marshal,' Joe Tonkin said equably, and there was a tight set to the big man's jaw as he watched Grit Harding charge out of the office and slam the door.

* * *

'Rider comin'!'

It was evening, and almost dark. They had spent the afternoon dozing in the shade, Guiana the more restless of the two as he drifted into sleep to ride down endless back-trails in search of a man bearing a grudge. Curtis Long also slept fitfully, committed now to helping John Guiana and deeply interested by what the horse rancher had let slip.

'*A tall man, eyes like an Injun; a Mex, handy with a saddle gun; a feller looked enough like me for Grit*

Harding to slam me in a strap-steel cell . . .'

The rider was approaching from the east, riding out of the deeper blackness that rolled across the endless plains in futile pursuit of the dying sun. Long had caught the sound of hoofbeats, rolled away from his saddle and was at the outer fringe of the trees with his six-gun ready.

Taking his time, knowing Long had the situation covered, Guiana moved twenty paces to his left and melted into the deep shadows. His six-gun rasped as he pulled it from stiff leather. One of the horses, the bay, stirred, nickered uneasily as it roused and caught the scent of the strange horse and, over at the edge of the woods, Long cursed softly.

By flattening himself to the carpet of dew-dampened leaves, Guiana was able to see through the trees. The night skies were already luminous and sprinkled with stars. Against them, the rider was a dark silhouette. He had caught the sound of Guiana's bay. Now he was motionless, sitting straight in the saddle as he listened, maybe even sniffed the air.

If he does, Guiana thought, he'll smell the fire; maybe has done already, caught it some ways off, been following it for human company and a bite to eat.

Then again he mused with a thin smile, he could be a scout for the posse, realizes he's ridden up on the two fugitives and can't see how the hell he's going to get away with his hide in one piece.

Curtis Long broke the impasse.

'Listen close, feller!'

He followed the shouted words with a deliberately noisy cocking of his pistol.

'Ain't no need for me to explain what you just heard. You're outlined against what light's left like a tall tree on rimrock, as easy to hit as a barn door. Don't make me do it. Step down, come on in leading your horse, your other hand reaching for the stars.'

For an instant, the man sat weighing his chances. Then Guiana let his breath go as the dark shape moved, seeming to drop out of the night skies as the man slid from the saddle. Twigs crackled as he walked in. His horse snorted, the bay answered, and Guiana knew that what he had taken for uneasiness had been recognition: the bay knew who was coming long before Guiana or Long.

'*Buenas noches*, Mig,' he called, and pushed himself up from the carpet of wet leaves as Curtis Long stepped to the smouldering fire and kicked it into life and the flames danced on the pale, apprehensive countenance of the Cash's Crossing hostler.

'Jesus Christ!' the Mexican said feelingly. 'You know I near to died of fright, John?'

In the dim light of Youngstown's saloon, Grit Harding's smashed hand was giving him hell. The pain of it was sending a raging river of fire all the way up his arm from the shattered bones and torn tendons. His right shoulder was the wall that took the onslaught of that pain. It was hunched awkwardly, a massive mound of muscle and bone balled up close to his thick neck as, with his left hand, he tossed back glass after glass of raw whiskey.

But instead of dulling the pain, the fiery spirit was adding fuel to the anger smouldering within the Cash's Crossing marshal.

'Johnny Guiana's gotta hang,' he said thickly.

'We're runnin' out of banks,' Sharpe Eagan said, 'and I'm worn to a frazzle chasin' my own tail over half of Texas.'

'And them two gunny-sacks stuffed with all that *dinero* we've been collecting,' said Tony Cruz with a flashing grin, 'they are bringing Eagan's horse to its knees.'

'Easiest way,' Eagan said bluntly, 'is a slug in the back, from ambush, and to hell with hangin'.'

'Now that,' said Cruz with a roll of his eyes, 'would give me much pleasure,' and metal rattled on woodwork as he proudly lifted the Winchester up in front of the bar where the light from the smoking oil lamps caught the highlights in its burnished metal.

Harding shook his head. 'Hangin's the only way,' he insisted. 'It's what we're gettin' paid for, and it's gotta be done legal.' He eased his right arm in its grubby sling, slid the empty jolt glass along the rough board bar to the bored bartender and said, 'Only thing is, Joe Tonkin's lettin' his brain talk him out of common sense. He now figures there's some doubt over who pulled them robberies. Says he knows Curt Long some, reckons the man wouldn't have plucked Guiana's neck from that hang rope without good reason.' He caught the glass as it came slopping back down the bar, narrowed his eyes and said, 'Ain't he a Starlight rider?'

'Comes and goes,' Eagan said, his eyes thoughtful.

'A strange fellow,' the Mexican agreed. 'A line-rider, sure, and a good one. But most times he walks around the spread with them blue eyes everywhere, sharp enough to cut clear through to a man's soul.'

Harding tossed back his drink, gasped, said hoarsely, 'Right now he's rode clear, him and Guiana. Last I saw they was headin' in a direction — if they held it — would take 'em close to Starlight. That happens, we're hock deep in bad trouble.'

'We?' Tony Cruz laughed. He looked around the almost empty saloon, lowered his voice to a conspiratorial whisper and said, 'Only trouble me and Sharpe's got is how to spend this cash when we make it across the border.'

'The hell!' Harding swore. 'We've got a job to finish.'

'You and Joe Tonkin,' Sharpe Eagan said easily. 'Lawmen both — and that makes everything legal, just the way you want it.'

Harding's glass slammed down on the bar. 'Didn't I just tell you Tonkin's holdin' off? Besides which, I don't need that Mormon do-gooder. What I need,' he went on, his eyes crafty, 'is three men makin' for the Mex border west of Starlight, by chance comin' across a fugitive from justice and stoppin' just long enough to do what's right and proper.'

Cruz shrugged. 'There is that possibility,' he said, and glanced at Sharpe Eagan.

'Renegin'' always did stick in my craw,' Eagan admitted, 'and if we're makin' for the border anyways . . . '

'Every one of you with good right hands to make up for this,' Harding said, and he lifted his bandaged hand, waggled it, swore again, softly, as fierce pain knifed.

'When?' Sharpe asked.

'Get it over with,' Harding gritted. 'Now's as good a time as any.'

'Con Shipley's over at the livery,' Sharpe said, and grinned. 'Looks too much like Guiana to show hisself.'

'Let's go,' Grit Harding said. 'And make damn sure you've got a rope.'

Boots pounded the boards, kicking

up dry sawdust as the three men turned and walked out through the swing doors.

★ ★ ★

The trouble arose, Joseph Tonkin decided, from knowing who and what to believe.

Grit Harding he didn't trust. His own eyes had never let him down, and he was willing to swear on the Book of Mormon that he'd seen the man he now knew to be John Guiana ride into town on a big blood bay, rob the bank, then half kill a young girl in his haste to get away.

Cigarette smoke drifted as the big Youngstown constable leaned back in his chair in the empty office and stared through narrowed eyes at the town's lamps glowing beyond the dark window.

Well, no, that wasn't all true.

He'd watched Guiana and his cronies ride in. Between then and the outbreak of violence, Tonkin recalled, he'd been over at the tonsorial for his morning shave, then passed the time of day with half a dozen townsfolk in and around the mercantile. The rattle of gunfire had alerted him. He'd charged out onto the plankwalk to see the three gunmen, hightailing, Guiana out front.

Tonkin frowned, mashed out his cigarette and swore softly as he realized he was swinging back and forth between the position he'd taken with Harding, belief in what his own eyes had told him, then nagging doubts that put him right back where he'd started.

He'd been more than fifty yards from the bank, the owlhoots already fifty yards on the far side of it and riding away from him. The lead rider was on a blood bay, a lean character wearing a black Stetson — but because, hours later, Guiana rode into town riding a similar horse and wearing similar clothes, was that clear enough identification for a lawman to drag a protesting stranger from his bath and organize a necktie party?

133

Well, Tonkin argued, jaw muscles bulging as fleeting images of a young girl falling under flashing hooves resurfaced and his dormant anger began to stir, why not? How many men rode blood bays of that quality? And of those — few in number, for sure — how many would, by some freak coincidence, be wearing the same black hat as the bank robber, the same clothes over the same lean frame, and ride into town on the same damn morning the bank was robbed?

'Nary a one,' Tonkin declared to the empty office, and he came out of his chair with a grunt that signified a decision reached.

No time to raise and swear in a posse of sleepy townsfolk so scared they'd likely fall out of the saddle, no reason to anyways. One man could ride unseen, unheard. One man would have surprise on his side.

John Guiana was last seen heading north-east, him and that Starlight rider.

Why Guiana had come back was a mystery, what made Curtis Long save him from hanging was another — but for sure they were both riding to join their owlhoot pards and make a run for the border with the hardearned cash stolen from the honest citizens of two Texas towns.

Eyes bleak, Tonkin unlocked the gun rack, selected a Remington 10-gauge shotgun, patted the six-gun at his hip and went out into the street. As he locked the door behind him he looked on past the saloon, saw four riders. A flash of white was revealed on an arm as they passed a swinging lantern, telling Tonkin all he needed to know.

Grit Harding. Heading back to Cash's Crossing. Or was he working something else of a devious nature, craftily heading one way but with his thinking elsewhere? Howsomever, he was heading out of town and that left Tonkin on his own, just the way he liked it.

With a feeling of satisfaction, Joe Tonkin stepped down off the plank-walk, climbed aboard his patiently waiting horse and swung it about until its nose pointed to Mexico.

10

'I am wanted for murder, in Nuevo Laredo,' Mig Angelo said. In the flickering light of the campfire his dark eyes flashed angrily. 'It was a mistake, a drunken *gringo* in a *cantina*, a gunshot in a crowded room. But Harding, he found out long, long ago.' He shrugged eloquently. 'So for a time I am his servant. What he wants, I do.'

'Like giving one bay horse to me, another to the man who looks like me but robs banks and murders a teller.'

'Sure. There was no choice. But all the while I knew that was betraying a good friend, John. I had stepped over a line, and what I had done sickened me. So now it is finished.'

'Yeah,' Guiana said. 'First time I saw the posse there was six men. Grit Harding reminded me, but I guess one kinda melted away somewhere between the Crossing and Youngstown.'

Angelo flashed a sly grin. 'I go along with Harding. He tol' me he needs men for a posse. I think, maybe if I ride with him for some way, there will come a chance.'

'Six men chasin' a killer,' Curtis Long said, nodding thoughtfully as he watched the hostler. 'Harding up front, those behind ridin' wide so they don't choke on his dust.'

'And then there was only five,' Angelo said, 'and if Harding bothered to count he was in too much of a hurry . . .'

'A clean break, just the way you wanted,' Guiana said. 'You'll make it to the border, Mig, drift south, find yourself a pretty *señorita*.'

'And you, John?'

'Guiana's got a shadow to chase,' Long said, and lifted an eyebrow as Guiana sensed something in the line-rider's voice and tossed him a glance.

'A hundred shadows from the past,' Guiana said softly, still watching Long, 'and every damn one of them gone like river mist when the sun comes up.'

'Maybe not all of 'em,' Curtis Long said. He tossed the makings across the fire and, as Guiana hitched himself up on an elbow and began rolling a smoke, the Starlight man went on, 'You saw those three bandits close up. If you described them right, there's a finger pointin' in a direction that don't come as too much of a surprise.'

'It bein'?'

'Starlight,' said Curtis Long, and the match's sudden flare revealed a glint of suppressed excitement in his eyes.

Mulling over Long's words, in particular the sudden dropping of Starlight into the conversation like a hard rock disturbing a placid pool where secrets had been long submerged, Guiana idly watched the Mexican drift away from the firelight to throw his rig over his bronc. Guiana and the Starlight line-rider had packed their gear and saddled up soon after Angelo arrived, figuring that while they were on their feet they might as well do something useful. Now, the Mexican hostler came back, twigs snapping under his boots, a thin black cheroot in his thin fingers and a lucifer forgotten in his hand as a troubled look creased his dark countenance.

'I spoke with Brad one week ago,' he said, his eyes on Long. 'He tol' me he had taken on a new hand . . .'

He seemed lost in thought as he struck the match, lit the cheroot, let the thin blue smoke drift to mask the glint in his eyes.

'Brad?' Guiana said.

'Brad Krane, Starlight ramrod,' Long said. He turned to the Mexican. 'How come you know Krane? It's usually me who rides to the Crossing. What was he doin' there?'

'Buying horses, selling horses.' Angelo's smile was white in the darkness, the conchos on his sombrero glinting as he shifted his weight, looked at Guiana.

'Back to them matching blood bays again,' John Guiana said bitterly, 'that

140

later came in handy when stolen Lazy B horses outlived their usefulness.'

'It was a business deal, John, nothing more. Like I tol' you, it was Harding forced my hand, Harding who drove me to this, a crazy run to the border.'

'Maybe Krane is clear,' Long mused. 'Those *banditos* stole your horses could be in this for reasons known only to themselves. I can name names, but what good will that do? You've already seen their faces, and drawn a blank.'

'Worth a try,' Guiana said. 'Things got kinda hazy, one man throwin' punches, another with a rifle muzzle rammed in my ear.'

'Him, I know,' Long said. 'If Krane told Angelo he'd recently hired a man, that'd be the Mex with the '73 Winchester. His name's Tony Cruz. The 'breed who's handy with his fists is Sharpe Eagan, the feller looks like you has to be Con Shipley.'

'Nope.' Guiana shook his head. He pondered for a moment, said, 'Those names don't mean a thing, so if they ain't workin' for their own ends and you reckon this Krane feller is in the clear — who's top dog at Starlight?'

'Ben Stone,' Long said, and waited.

Guiana shook his head. 'A name like that, I could've come across it a dozen or more times without it registerin'. But I'll stick my neck out, I've never met the man, never heard of him.'

'He's a feller crawled bare-naked out of a tarpaper shack and in a lifetime of struggle clawed his way to the top,' Long said. 'Biggest damn rancher in mid-Texas, sixtyish, vain, treats his purty wife no better than a slave, a fancy-Dan known for wearin' pearl-grey Stetsons and a blue bandanna knotted around his neck to hide the wrinkles of comin' old age.'

'Would seem to rule him out,' Guiana said, 'unless to scrape together some cash on his way up he rode the owlhoot for a spell, held up a few stages, maybe robbed a bank.'

'You did,' Long pointed out.

'Small stuff, yeah — but all this,'

Guiana said, 'to get even for something I don't even recall? Those three fellers pullin' bank robberies, then the Crossing marshal's involved, maybe that Mormon feller, Joe Tonkin?'

Mig Angelo coughed in the darkness, sending sparks showering from the thin cheroot. 'Maybe,' he said, suddenly uneasy, 'now we're ready to go we should do our thinking some place else.'

'You hear something?' Catlike, the lean Starlight rider was up on his feet and prowling his head turned towards the open land beyond the trees.

'I hear nothing,' Angelo said, too quickly. 'But when Harding realizes John is no longer in Youngstown, he'll keep riding, swing his posse north, push them to the limit ... '

'Grit Harding got hisself shot up,' John Guiana said. On his feet, one eye on the tense, watchful Starlight rider, in a few terse sentences he told Mig Angelo all that had occurred since his clean break from the posse. 'I almost

143

got hanged,' he concluded. 'and let me tell you, I can't think of nothing worse.'

'Unless,' Mig Angelo said with a curious, twisted smile, 'you got hanged, but cut down before you died. How you like to choke for a while, eh, John?'

Guiana shivered. 'Count me out, Mig.' He shrugged. 'Anyhow, Long rode up before the party'd really got goin', then Harding got his hand shot away and never managed to wield his quirt on that big bay. But with my life at stake you know I ain't likely to stop searchin' for the man behind this madness, and Grit — '

'Grit Harding's a lawman driven by greed,' Curtis Long said, stepping back into the circle of firelight. 'The badge pinned to his vest says what he's doin' is legal, but that's only half the story. If he is gettin' paid, he'll be paid for results. The other side of the coin is failure, and with the truth out it's him'll be doin' the paying, in time spent in the Pen and — '

Again he broke off, watching the

jittery Mexican. Canting his head sideways, he listened hard, then nodded, his face grim.

'Yeah,' Mig Angelo said shakily. 'Now we both hear something, eh, Long? Riders. Heading this way.'

11

They were moving at breakneck speed, coming from two directions out of the thin moonlight, dark shapes with the glint of metal in their fists and the only sound the terrible thunder of hooves.

'Move 'em back!' Guiana shouted, and followed his cry with a rush to where the big bay tossed its head nervously. Within seconds his and Long's horse were out of the glade and tethered deep in the woods. Then the two men spun about, diving for cover as a volley of shots rang out and hot lead whined overhead and snicked through the high branches.

'What the hell — !'

Long snapped a fast glance at the approaching riders, then twisted his head to peer back into the woods.

There, clawing his way into the saddle, Angelo shouted breathlessly,

'Maybe some of those men ride around the flank. I head them off — '

Underbrush crackled as the Mexican dug in his spurs, spun the bronc and forced it to flee from the onrushing attackers through the thickest of the timber, the lunging animal's ears flattened in fear as gunfire crackled.

'You trust that feller enough to have him at your back?'

'It was his horse got me this far,' Guiana said. He jerked his head instinctively as a slug thumped into a tree alongside his face. 'Time we split up,' he said, 'lie low. They picked up the scent of woodsmoke, maybe saw the glow from the fire. But that's it. For all they know, we could be long gone.'

'Could be diggin' ourselves into a hole. We give 'em time they'll be all around us — and I don't trust that Mex.'

'Forget Mig. Watch these fellers. We split, they'll need to do the same to root us out.'

Long grunted agreement in the

darkness, said, 'Just don't get boxed in,' then moved away to the left at a snaking, crouching run into the trees. He stopped — in Guiana's estimation — no more than thirty yards away, sank to the ground. As he did so a rider reached the fringe of the woods over to Guiana's right and came out of the saddle in a plunging dive that took him into cover. Tall. Dark eyes and high cheekbones catching the weak light. A pistol gleaming in a gloved fist.

And, unconsciously, Guiana's hand went up to his face where this man's hard fists had made their mark.

The rider melted into the shadows with an Indian's stealth. Guiana moved silently backwards. He took a line angling away from the gunman, pistol high and cocked. Before each step his booted feet cautiously tested the ground. His free hand carefully brushed trailing branches aside.

According to Long, the 'breed was Sharpe Eagan. That left Shipley and the Mex — and Grit Harding. But Harding was maimed. And what about Youngstown's Mormon constable, Joe Tonkin?

Even as the thoughts raced through his mind Guiana saw two riders bearing down on Long's position, another high up the slope with his bulk outlined against the night skies. Grit Harding — or Tonkin?

He shook his head angrily. Brush crackled to his right, and he held his breath, squinting into the blackness under the trees. Then the thud of hooves away to his left drew his gaze. The two riders were abreast of Long's position — but still came on. And the man to his right, Eagan, had gone silent and still.

Don't get boxed, Long had said. With a worm of unease stirring in his guts, Guiana recalled the Starlight rider's warning about Mig Angelo. And now the two riders had pulled their broncs to a halt and were out of the saddle.

Under the black Stetson that had branded John Guiana a murdering bank robber, Con Shipley's face gleamed white as he turned his head. As he did so, the man on the skyline whistled a soft, keening note, and a hand rose, cut down.

Left hand. That made the bulky figure Grit Harding.

Both men slipped into the woods.

John Guiana cursed silently.

From high up the slope, the watcher was looking down on trees bathed in thin moonlight — and he had picked up movement. Directed by Harding, instead of separating to hunt down both men all three had converged to go after one. But they'd know the location of both, and the man watching from the high ground would make it difficult for Curtis Long to make a move.

Still angling deeper into the trees, Guiana was forced to watch three directions. Shipley was coming on slow, but as straight as an arrow. The Mexican — Cruz? — was circling, putting himself between Guiana and Long. Eagan was now on the move, forming the second jaw of a contracting pincer. If Guiana let it close . . .

But, he reasoned with himself, all they knew of his position was an approximation. In the woods they were walking blind, the watcher on the high ground useless. They could walk close, damn near tread on him without seeing.

Like an animal settling for the night, John Guiana sank to the ground, wriggled deep, curled himself under a thicket.

The noise of their approach was eerie, bodily movements undetectable by the sharpest of ears, yet the rasp of their tense breathing in the still night air converging on his hiding place like the soughing of the uneasy wind presaging a storm. Up on the hillside, Harding's bronc whinnied, and Guiana thought of the friendly blood bay, and held his breath.

A boot touched his ankle, kicked at what a man figured was a rock.

'You take a look at the fire?'

'Near dead.'

Question and answer; tall silhouettes against pale skies. Two men, Con Shipley and Sharpe Eagan, their clothing brushing against the concealing thicket, snagging on thorns. A third, closing in.

'They have lit out,' this third man said, and it was the Mexican who had circled left. 'I could smell coffee, cigarettes — but they have gone, I tell you.'

'Hell, wasn't Angelo supposed to watch out for them?'

'He rode north, sure. But he tol' me, if he finds them he will stick like a burr.' Cruz chuckled softly. 'Is easy. That Guiana, he trusts Angelo like a brother.'

The boot moved, a heel ground down hard to pinch the skin of Guiana's calf with painful force, and he clenched his teeth.

'Maybe he does,' Eagan said, 'but what the hell is he playin' at?'

A match flared as he lit a cigarette.

And knowing that in the dark night all three men were now as good as blind, Guiana let his jaw muscles relax, smiled a thin smile.

'What would you do,' Con Shipley said, 'if you'd robbed two banks, killed a man, escaped hangin' by a slice of luck?'

'Luck?' Eagan eased away from the thicket, noisily blew smoke. 'That Texas Ranger tailed Harding and Tonkin out of town, was in the right place because he put himself there. If I was alone, in Guiana's boots, I'd be far west knockin' back tequila in some smoky *cantina*. But backed by Long, a hunch tells me he might just be closin' in . . .'

'Is no matter. We don' work for Starlight no more. We have give it one last try, now Harding can do his own dirty work — '

'That's up to you.' Eagan's voice cut through the Mexican's words. 'Me, I figure I'm in debt; a pass through Starlight to raise the alarm won't do no harm.'

The boot left Guiana's leg. The three men drifted away, their voices clear, but fading. Eventually, there was the creak of leather, the jingle of a bridle, the lazy thud of hooves as the Starlight men rode their horses away at a walk.

'Cut through the woods,' Curtis Long said, close by, and John Guiana rolled from under the thicket and regained his feet. 'Left Harding contemplatin' his folly, wonderin' how he's gonna rope you and hang you, all on his lonesome with one smashed hand.'

'You move like a ghost wearin' a dark coat at midnight, Ranger.'

Long chuckled. 'Yeah, quite a surprise, that comin' out. I reckon Eagan's sharper than I figured.'

'Him and his pards. If they know you've got a badge stashed, it'll be common knowledge at Starlight.'

It seemed that Long pondered on that as they picked their way through the trees, careful to remain under cover as they returned to the horses. On the way, Guiana glanced up the long slope. No bulky figure broke the sharp curve of the skyline.

'Don't mean we can relax,' Long said, catching the glance. 'A cagey lawman'd do what was necessary, then drop down the lee slope so's only his hat's showin' and keep his eyes peeled from there. Wisest option in the circumstances is for us to take Angelo's route through the woods, along the river — that's if you're ridin' with me to Starlight?'

'Speakin' of Angelo,' Guiana said, poised with a hand on the horn and one foot thrust into a stirrup, 'right now I can't think of anyone who'd be comin' back through the woods exceptin' that lyin' Mex hostler.'

'Well, glory be!' Curtis Long breathed.

12

Joe Tonkin watched it all.

He caught the rattle of gunfire while riding some way to the west of the action, immediately spurred his horse towards where muzzle flashes winked red in the thin moonlight. He skirted the west flank of a slope, rode past a stand of trees and instinctively drew rein as a still, mounted figure was revealed, high up to his right.

Grit Harding. And downslope, clearly visible, three riders closing in on a stand of cottonwoods — and one of them wearing a black hat and riding a familiar blood bay.

Tonkin drew a breath, held it while he counted to ten, let it out with a snort of frustration.

He'd spent an hour in his office, brow furrowed, got it all worked out before he left Youngstown. Harding was heading back to Cash's Crossing with the remains of his posse. Guiana and Long were joining their owlhoot pards then riding west to the border.

So, what the hell was John Guiana doing pouring hot lead into a stand of cottonwoods, watched by a marshal whose posse was noticeably absent and who, even as Tonkin watched, stirred himself enough to whistle thin and clear and raise his arm in an obvious signal.

Harding, in cahoots with Guiana?

What, in the name of Lucifer, was going on?

In his mind, Joe Tonkin backtracked.

Guiana had pleaded his innocence, had been backed up by the Starlight line-rider, Curtis Long. But Tonkin had seen a man on a blood bay ride into Youngstown and rob the bank, had seen the same man ride in again, and promptly arrested him.

John Guiana.

Or was it?

Second time, when he'd taken a bath — most definitely.

But what about the first time?

If the man now dismounted and slipping stealthily into the cottonwoods with his pards and getting the full cooperation of Grit Harding was Guiana, nothing made sense. If, however, he was the bank robber — but not Guiana — then everything began to fall into place.

For some reason, Harding wanted John Guiana out of the way. If both bank robberies were set up to achieve that end, then Harding was crooked. If Harding was crooked he was in cahoots, not with the innocent Guiana, but with the owlhoots. So what Joe Tonkin was witnessing was three owlhoots hunting somebody who'd either holed up in the cottonwoods, or been caught there with his pants around his ankles.

John Guiana.

It had to be — and Joe Tonkin had spent an hour reaching the wrong conclusion.

He was still silently berating himself

for his incompetence when the three men came back out of the cottonwoods, mounted up, and rode through the edge of the woods in a northerly direction. When he glanced up the slope, Grit Harding had melted into the night.

No more gunfire, which suggested that the owlhoots had wasted a heap of hot lead.

With a sigh, Joe Tonkin rode down the slope to take a look.

13

It was an hour past midnight when they rode into Starlight, trailing fine dust as they passed under the high beam over the gates, their weary broncs lifting their heads to the clear fresh scent of the Pecos. The big yard was empty, the pole corrals like frameworks of white bone in the moonlight. The only other light was the warm glow from single lanterns burning in one window of the main house and in the open door of the bunkhouse.

'Brad Krane's got his orders,' Sharpe Eagan said, his breath misty in the cool air. 'Any word comes in, he carries it to Stone — no matter what the time.'

'We got news, all right,' Con Shipley said. 'Guiana's on the loose, and Curtis Long's shown his colours.'

'Yeah,' said Tony Cruz, 'and don't forget Stone's short three good hands.'

'Not yet he ain't.'

Cruz flicked a glance at the 'breed, opened his mouth to object then clamped it shut as Eagan pulled in close to the bunkhouse, slid from the saddle and threw a loose hitch around the pole. The others were following suit when the lamplight was blotted out as a figure appeared in the doorway.

'Took you long enough.'

Eagan laughed. He walked up to the tall foreman, stood before him with his thumbs hooked loosely into his gunbelts.

'Robbin' two banks takes some time.'

'Two?' Brad Krane slammed a lean, stiff arm across the entrance as Cruz and Shipley tried to step inside. 'This'd better be good, Eagan.'

The 'breed sighed as his companions backed off, the wrangler's foot sending a bucket clattering. 'Guiana was picked up by Harding after the first, broke jail, headed west. We pulled the same trick in Youngstown. This time Harding and Joe Tonkin got a rope looped over a

161

branch, the noose around Guiana's neck.'

Krane stirred, stretched to his full height, nodded. 'Right. So I walk over, tell Stone the job's done.'

'Wrong.' Eagan shook his head.

'I warned you this'd better be good,' Krane said. His cold blue eyes lifted to look beyond Eagan. When the 'breed followed the foreman's gaze he saw a figure on the gallery of the ranch house, silently watching.

His own eyes shifted sideways to meet Con Shipley's; almost imperceptibly, he nodded.

'Curtis Long stepped in,' Eagan said, and saw the foreman's eyes narrow. 'Hell, Stone knew Long was a Ranger, knew why he was playin' line-rider while he poked around. So for six months he backed off, played the honest rancher.'

'Get to the point.'

Eagan sneered. 'What he did, he let a personal vendetta waste all that good work. He's no closer to Guiana and

162

Long's got something on him, given to him on a plate without bothering diggin' up evidence of phoney water rights, protection money taken at gunpoint without guarantees.'

'Only if someone talked.'

'Oh, no!' Eagan grinned at the tall foreman, knowing that Shipley and Cruz had changed position and were behind him, to his left and right. 'Angelo did his job, and he's still out there. Harding took a slug, still kept tryin'. Us?' Eagan chuckled. 'We're on our way to the border, ain't seen hide nor hair of Guiana or Long, only stopped by to give you the news — '

'And now you're staying to see this through to its conclusion.'

The new voice was bleak, and now it was Krane's turn to grin. He looked across at Ben Stone, at the shotgun in his massive hands, at the two cowed gunslingers who had stepped aside as the rancher came silently across the yard.

'If no one talked, Long's got exactly

what he left with, and that's nothing. If he rides in with John Guiana, then Guiana dies.' The fire glowing in Stone's dark-brown eyes was threatening to become an inferno, the hard mouth a razor-slash, the heavy jaw bunched with muscle.

'He dies, and I don't care how. It was appropriate for him to hang. If he's that slippery, let's see if he can slip away from four men with six-guns, another with a shotgun who will take great pleasure in blasting his head off his shoulders.'

'And the Ranger?'

Now it was Stone's turn to grin at a surly Sharpe Eagan, the twisted grimace leaving his eyes aflame with fury.

'What damn Ranger!' He spat the words. 'A man announces himself, or pays the consequences. Curtis Long rides line for Starlight, that's the limit of my knowledge. He sides with Guiana, he's a traitor.'

'Amen to that,' said Brad Krane.

Eagan shrugged. To Ben Stone he

said, 'I guess with that scattergun you can force us to hang around. But that don't mean either one of us'll lift a pistol to back your play.'

'With us or against us,' Krane said grimly. 'Ben can't afford to face Guiana with three men at his back he don't trust with his life.'

Tony Cruz spat, the wet globule hitting the dust close to Stone's shiny boots. 'Tell your boss,' he said to Krane, 'a twelve-gauge pointin' at a man's belt buckle buys hate, not loyalty.'

Stone's grin was savage. 'And tell that goddamn Mex,' he said to Krane, 'this shotgun, one way or another, easy or hard, bequeaths to me those gunny-sacks slung behind Eagan's saddle.'

'The hell — !' Eagan took a step, his eyes narrowed, both hooked hands hovering over packed holsters.

'All right!'

Stone's words cracked like a pistol shot. In the same instant he nodded to Brad Krane, who moved across to unhitch Sharpe Eagan's bronc and loop the reins around his wrist.

'This gets us nowhere.' Stone's voice was taut, his eyes watchful; the shotgun lined up rock-steady on Eagan's belly. 'Threats and counter-threats don't make sense when what we're arguing over is a man none of you know, another who's spent six months watching every damn one of us like a hawk after blood.'

'Your blood, not mine,' Eagan said. 'In six months, Curt Long has made a lot of friends.'

'So now those friends have got a choice to make,' Ben Stone said softly. 'A man whose loyalty is questionable, against a pony carryin' two loaded gunny-sacks that Krane's about to lock away in the barn. You play along, you'll get them back, the promise of a clear ride to the border.'

'And time's running out,' Brad Krane said flatly. 'When John Guiana gets here he'll be lookin' for the men who ruined his life — and right now, that don't include Ben Stone.'

Tony Cruz swore softly, his eyes glittering.

Eagan let his breath go through his nostrils.

An uneasy silence settled.

★ ★ ★

'You persist in this,' she said. 'I'll walk out and never come back.'

The soft lamplight gleamed in her hair. He drank from a glass of cut crystal, his dark eyes becoming as hard as his name as he heard the determination in her voice, saw the threat in eyes that in their grim determination were a match for his own.

'There will be some shooting,' he said quietly. 'I want you to stay at the back of the house, don't — '

'You're not even listening.'

'Do I ever?' He shrugged. 'You've sent the children to town, why should you be worried?'

Her laugh was suddenly brittle.

'It's you who should be worried. I said I'll walk out, and I mean it — '

'Running away from prosperity?'

'From misery.'

'You'll be back.'

'There'll be nothing to come back to.' She saw his frown, went on relentlessly, 'Because when I go the children will go with me, and I'll make damn sure that you're in no position to follow — ever!'

14

'I don' understand,' Mig Angelo protested. 'You are in the woods, afraid for your life, you hear some fellers talk an' right away you don' trust the only man help you escape the Crossing.'

'Talkin' amongst themselves,' Guiana said. 'Casual talk, they had no idea I was listenin', had no reason to lie.'

'A man hightails, leaves his pards when the goin' gets rough,' Curtis Long said along the barrel of his rifle, 'don't exactly inspire confidence in his integrity.'

Leather creaked as Angelo shifted uneasily in the saddle.

'I tol' you. If one of those fellers ride aroun' the side, I pick him off. I was wrong, is no matter.' His teeth flashed in a wide grin. 'You think I'm gonna come back if I'm what you say . . . a traitor?'

'I think you knew what you were doin' when you gave out two blood bays, not just the one,' Guiana said. 'To me, everything that happened then and now points to those fellers bein' friends of yours.'

'Johnny, Johnny,' Mig Angelo said soothingly. 'I run a livery stable. A man rides in with cash, I sell him a good horse. A little later my friend comes walking down the runway, in a hurry to get out of town, I do the same with no thought of payment.'

Guiana took a breath, flicked a glance at Curtis Long. They were in the small clearing, their horses ground-hitched where they had left them when they heard Angelo riding in. Long was backed into the trees with his rifle almost casually trained on the little Mexican. Guiana was standing along-side Angelo's horse, one restraining hand tight on a cheek strap. The burnt wood scent of the dying fire added its bite to air that was chill in the nostrils. The moon was veiled by high, thin cloud. A coyote called, the cry rising, then trailing into silence.

'Someone comin',' Curtis Long said.

He swung around. The steel rifle barrel glittered as he turned to face the new threat. Eyes narrowed, he threw down on the opening in the trees beyond which lay the open high ground. Guiana cursed softly, dipped his free hand to his holster. Even as he did so, Mig Angelo was swinging away. The bronc squealed as the Mexican raked its flanks with sharp spurs. Its eyes rolled white, its head jerked up. Guiana's hand was ripped from the cheekstrap. He staggered back, off balance. With his sombrero whipped off by the breeze and dangling from its neck cord, for the second time that night the Crossing hostler urged his bronc forward and sent it crashing through the trees.

'Joe Tonkin,' Guiana said, eyeing the dark shape of the oncoming rider, teeth clenched tight as he rubbed his hand. 'Recognize him anywhere. After what that lawman did I'll be seein' his black frock coat in my dreams.'

'Let him come,' Long said, 'we could do with an extra gun. Angelo's likely to blow this whole thing apart — if it was ever in one piece.'

'We sure won't take Starlight by surprise,' Guiana acknowledged, and with sudden decision he stepped fully into the patch of thin moonlight, his hands well clear of his thighs.

The big Youngstown lawman rode in with leather slapping and Spanish rowels jingling, his black eyes gleaming as they took in John Guiana then flicked to the lean line-rider standing back in the shadows. He grunted, drew rein, stepped down heavily.

'If that's a blood bay I'm lookin' at,' Tonkin said, 'I guess I owe somebody an apology.'

'Which words'd sound pretty hollow if I'd got to that necktie party five minutes later,' Long said.

Tonkin shrugged. 'A man spends his time thinkin' in ifs and maybes he'd have no time left for livin' anyhow.'

'Hell,' Guiana said with a grin, 'a philosophizin' Mormon.'

'But I ain't no mindreader,' Tonkin said, 'so would you mind tellin' me what the hell's goin' on!'

'Someone's intent on framin' Guiana, gettin' him strung up,' Long said. 'You must have figured that by now.'

'Let's say a talk with Grit Harding back in town didn't ease my mind none.'

'What you maybe don't know is all the signs point to Starlight.'

Long came out of the shadows, rifle in the crook of his left arm, slipped his hand into his vest pocket and brought out a gleaming badge in the shape of a star in a circle, pinned it to his vest front.

'Ben Stone?' Tonkin looked at the glittering badge, narrowed his eyes. 'Now, why would Ben do that — and iffen he did, why would someone houndin' a feller spent most of his adult life ridin' the owlhoot bring out the Texas Rangers?'

'Well, that's another story,' Long said, 'but my guess is puttin' the man fixin' to kill John Guiana behind bars could be like killin' two birds with the one load of buckshot.' He rammed the rifle into its boot, swung up into the saddle.

'And you still figure Starlight?'

'If you came down from that rise you must've seen that second blood bay,' John Guiana said.

'So?'

'The man ridin' it robbed two banks. Which way was he headed?'

Tonkin shrugged. 'Starlight's just one spread between here and the North Pole.'

'For Christ's sake!' Long said fiercely.

With a look of disgust, Guiana stepped up into the saddle, swung the bay hard around.

'All right.' Tonkin took hold of his saddle horn, paused with the reins in his hand to look calculatingly at

174

Guiana. 'I listened to Harding in town, then rode all this way to watch him set up on that slope while those fellers tried to flush you out. Seems to me if he'd wanted you for lawful reasons he'd still be on your tail. But, one way or another, he's dumped whatever the hell's goin' on in my lap . . . '

He swung over leather, clicked his tongue, eased the big horse forward.

'One thing,' Curtis Long said. 'A feller just rode out is sure to spill the beans unless we run him down.'

'So what the hell are we waitin' for?'

'Sure,' said John Guiana, and his smile was bleak. 'We know where the damn place is at — so let's ride for Starlight.'

15

It was Ben Stone who caught the first glimpse of the approaching rider, his eyes narrowed in both simmering anger and a degree of puzzlement as he saw the single figure emerge from a distant gully and cut hard and fast across the open ground between him and Starlight.

The moon had drifted behind thin high cloud; the skies were strangely luminous. In the eerie light the single rider, desperately spurring his horse, dragged a plume of dust. Then, as the distance swiftly narrowed, it was possible to catch the shine of silver winking on the man's broad-brimmed hat, and Stone grunted, knowing that the rider was the Cash's Crossing hostler, Miguel Angelo.

Alongside him on the ranch house's gallery, his wife said carefully, 'I can understand the reasons behind your . . . firm handling of neighbouring ranchers.' She smiled with genuine amusement at her tactful choice of words. Then the smile faded and she continued, 'But there's something going on that I don't understand. It involves Brad, and those three men I have never trusted. But I care nothing for them, no, not even for Brad Krane, even if he has been your right-hand man for more years than I can count and so contributed to our . . . prosperity. No, it's the children I care for, Ben. But something tells me that, whatever this obsession is that's taken hold of you, it is putting my family at risk — and I cannot condone it.'

'Nobody asked you to,' Stone said bluntly, and with a final glance at the approaching rider he took the steps down from the gallery, skirted the buckboard standing in front of the house and set off across the yard.

He was met halfway by Krane, and Sharpe Eagan.

'Angelo,' Krane said tersely. 'Maybe a mile of open space between him and three riders came out that arroyo doin' their damnedest to hang on his tail.'

'Three?'

'Guiana and Long,' Eagan said, watching the big rancher. 'After that it's anybody's guess.'

'Get Shipley and the Mex.'

'I told you,' Eagan said tightly, 'if Long's thirstin' for blood it's yours, not mine.'

Stone remained silent. He flicked a glance at the barn where Krane had stashed the two gunny-sacks, saw Eagan's lips tighten, the sullen tilt of his head that told him greed was overpowering caution. 'Go get Shipley and Cruz. Then all three of you get out of sight. Watch like hawks. You get a signal, come out with guns blazing.'

'Yeah,' Sharpe Eagan said, his head oddly tilted, high cheekbones catching the light as he eyed the rancher. 'Yeah, Stone, you give a signal and we'll come out, just like you say . . . '

He swung on his heel, headed for the bunkhouse and, as he did so, two shadowy figures drifted away from the doorway and fell in on either side of the 'breed. They stood talking, the murmur of their voices too soft for words to be distinguished. Then Eagan headed for the dilapidated outbuidings beyond the corral to the left of the gates, Shipley and Cruz crossing the yard to a stand of trees on the opposite side.

'I don't trust them,' Brad Krane said.

'You're the second person in as many minutes to tell me that,' Stone said, his head turned to the swelling sound of hoofbeats. 'Only trust's got nothing to do with tonight's work, Krane. Tonight's work is about retribution. And those three black-hearted hellions will stand by me or, by God, they'll pay the price alongside John Guiana.'

The thunder of hoofbeats changed to a clatter as the approaching rider tore in through Starlight's wide gate and onto the hard-packed earth of the yard.

He came across at the gallop, was skidding to a halt as Ben Stone reached him; tumbling from the saddle with his old Sharpes single-shot clutched in one hand when Stone grabbed a cheek strap and held the lathered horse with an iron grip; then spilling a torrent of words that brought a flush of anger to the rancher's face and sent Brad Krane across the yard at a fast jog.

'Joe Tonkin?' Stone said with disbelief. 'Are you telling me that goddamn Ranger Long has got Tonkin twisted around his little finger?'

'I tell you nothing for certain.' Angelo's eyes were wild, his face glistening with sweat. 'But I saw him once, when I look back. No mistake.'

'Guiana will have told him a tale,' Stone said. 'Must've been enough to rouse the Ranger's suspicions, get Tonkin thinking about that badge he totes, the duties he's being paid to carry out.'

'Makes no difference,' Angelo said,

his grin suddenly wolfish. 'We kill John Guiana anyhow, eh, Ben?'

'Yeah,' Ben Stone said. 'We'll sure as hell kill him, *amigo* — law or no goddamn law!'

16

They caught one glimpse of him, an indistinct figure bent over the neck of a gutsy, tireless mount chosen by a man who worked with horses and had selected the best. Then they were gone, dark and distant shapes on which the sheen of sweat glistened in the pale light of the moon, a long shadow with a raking stride abruptly swallowed up like a gopher disappearing down a hole by the deeper shadows in the lee of a high, rocky knoll.

'No chance of catchin' him!' Curtis Long yelled from some way back.

'Even if we do, it's too late,' Guiana called over his shoulder, easing back to allow the Ranger's lean mount to draw level with the powerful bay. 'Mig won't give up without a fight,' he told Long, 'and the sound of gunfire'll bring every man at Starlight tumblin' out of his bunk.'

'That ain't many,' Long said. 'Spring round-up ain't started. What you've seen so far is about what you're up against.'

'Them three, plus Stone and his ramrod.' Guiana nodded, mentally adding Mig Angelo to the hard bunch he was facing. Still thinking, he slowed the bay to an easy walk. As Joe Tonkin rode up, he and Long drifted a few yards apart to make way for the big Mormon constable.

'Ain't seen so many people around since last summer's county fair,' Tonkin grumbled, and when both men glanced sharply at him he said, 'Him up ahead, two riders some ways back, clingin' like burrs.'

'Any guesses?'

'Harding?' He cocked an eye at the waiting Guiana, then said, 'I figured he was bound for the Crossing, but it looks like he ain't given up on you after all.'

'Or the *dinero* promised him by

Stone — if he's the man back of all this.'

'Oh, it's Stone all right,' Long said. 'A man don't spend six months on a spread where something bad's cookin' without pickin' up some of the smell.'

Guiana grimaced. 'That bad?'

'Bad enough.' Long sniffed the air as they crossed the line of Angelo's hurried flight and, doing the same as they jogged in the lee of the knoll, Guiana turned aside to spit out the raw taste of the Mexican's dust.

'I ain't seen Stone jawin' with those three tore into you,' Long went on, 'but that's because he uses Brad Krane to carry messages. He's a family man, puts on a front with expensive clothes and that fancy hat; got a lot to lose — '

'Yeah,' Guiana cut in bitterly, 'that makes him and me. And if that is Harding out there it looks like we've rode into the jaws of a pincer that'll close tighter than an alligator's jaw.'

Joe Tonkin had been riding along

listening closely, his black form jouncing heavily in the saddle. Now, above the rattle of hooves as they clattered away from the shadow of the knoll, he said, 'Ain't nothing I've heard suggests any reason for Stone wantin' you dead. I mentioned a while back I owed somebody an apology, which was kind of a crafty way of puttin' it, because I mentioned no names. Let's just say right now I'm sittin' on the fence. Before the night's out, someone, somewhere is likely to come up with something tips me one way or tother, an' — '

'Are you sayin' I'm still not in the clear?' Guiana demanded angrily, for the first time noting the Remington 10-gauge rammed into the big constable's saddle boot.

'What I'm sayin' is when I do jump,' Tonkin said easily, 'I aim to jump on the guilty man.'

'One thing I neglected to mention,' Long said, 'is hidin' under that bandanna Stone wears — along with the wrinkles — is something that looks mighty like the scars a man'd get if he dangled for too long from a hang rope.' He flicked a glance at Guiana. 'Mean anything?'

'Only that those scars'd be around my neck without me knowin' a thing about it if you hadn't rode up when you did.'

'Which ain't much help in findin' out who's tellin' the truth,' Tonkin said drily.

'You won't have much longer to wait,' said Curtis Long.

They had reached the crest of a rise that fell away from them to the north-west in a long, gradual incline. On the flat plain clearly visible in the eerie light cast by the veiled moon, warm lights glowed.

They had reached Starlight.

17

The first shot winged towards them as they rode through the gates to Starlight, the flat slap of the rifle followed immediately by the soft whirr of a bullet displacing the air above the crown of Guiana's Stetson. The muzzle-flash betrayed the gunman's position, the logs at the corner of the bunkhouse briefly rimmed with fire as the echoes died.

'Look behind you,' Long said quietly.

Guiana turned to see Grit Harding and his partner stationed a hundred yards back, a hundred yards apart, sitting motionless in the saddle.

'Ain't gonna move unless Stone looks to be in trouble.'

'That figures,' Joe Tonkin said scathingly. 'If all lawmen was like that gutless bastard . . .'

He left the insult hanging, turned to

face the ranch and roared, 'Put that goddamn rifle away and allow the law to ride in and talk.'

'What law?' came the sardonic reply.

'Ben Stone,' Long said, 'over at the ranch house,' and Tonkin nodded.

'Quit playin' the fool, Ben. Three of your men're wanted for bank robbery and murder. You hand them over that'll be the end of it, you and your family can go back to sleep.'

'No, sir. The man robbed those banks is the man riding stirrup with you, the man who perfected the art during twenty years riding the owlhoot. Bring him along to the house, we'll string him up for you.'

'There'll be no — '

'Throw down your guns and hand over John Guiana, Tonkin, or the next slug'll part your hair two inches lower than you like it.'

'Now see here — '

The rifle cracked. Guiana heard the slug hit home, heard the strangled grunt as Joe Tonkin tilted sideways in the saddle, gloved hands grabbing for the horn. On the constable's far side, Curt Long drove his horse in close, took the big lawman's weight with his shoulder and eased him upright.

'I'm OK.' Breath whistled through Tonkin's nostrils as his jaw clamped shut. 'But we're stuck out here like flies waitin' to be swatted,' he said through his teeth. 'Nowhere to hide, nowhere to run.'

'The light's bad.' Guiana said. 'If we give him fast moving targets he won't have it so easy.'

'What about it, Joe?' Still supporting the constable, Long looked across at Guiana, gave a faint shake of the head. But the almost imperceptible movement was detected, and Tonkin snorted.

'A slug bit a chunk out of my shoulder. Take more than that to slow down Joe Tonkin.' He lifted his head, spat, shook off Curt Long and said, 'You aimin' to ride straight at 'em, scare 'em to death?'

Guiana chuckled drily. 'Harding's

189

back of us, that feller Stone and his ramrod out front. I ain't seen any sign of the 'breed and his pards, but I reckon they're pluggin' the gaps on either side . . . ' He shook his head. 'In different circumstances a wise man'd maybe ride home, sleep what's left of the night away, hope to hell a workable idea'd come with the dawn. But they've got us hemmed in all around so, yeah, one way's as good as another.' He dipped a hand, drew and cocked his six-gun in one smooth movement and said, 'I'm for ridin' on the house.'

Leather rasped as Tonkin slid the shotgun out of its boot. He reached back, groaned softly with pain, found a handful of cartridges in his saddlebag and straightened to put two between his teeth and the rest in his pocket.

With a jerk of his head he faced front, cocked the shotgun. Sweat made his countenance as shiny as his old frock-coat; his eyes were red with pain but flashing fire. In one sweep of his powerful legs he raked the bronc with his spurs. Then he was away, jerking back in the saddle as the bronc took off in a violent lunge and hammered across the yard.

'Jesus!' John Guiana said. 'So that's how it's done.'

The rifle was spitting fire from the corner of the bunkhouse when he spurred the bay after the big constable. Curt Long was yelling crazily behind him, then drawing level with his lean face split by a wild grin. Slugs kicked up dust ahead of them as they rounded the skeletal poles of the corral, and Guiana knew Grit Harding had moved closer and opened fire. Muzzle flashes lit the front of the ranch-house. Bullets plucked at Guiana's sleeve. A window went with a tinkle of breaking glass. Somewhere in the house light flared brightly as a lamp's glass chimney took a slug and the draught sent smoky flame leaping high. In the sudden glare, Guiana saw two crouched figures on the gallery. Then the light went out as someone used a blanket to extinguish the flame. In the same instant, the blood bay took a slug and Guiana went over its head to hit the dirt with a thud as the big horse went down.

His jaw snapped shut. Blood was a coppery taste wet on his lips, slick on his neck from the reopened gash on his ear. He spat dust, rolled, snapped a shot at the gallery that brought a torrent of curses in a voice he recognized.

Mig Angelo!

Then Joe Tonkin's shotgun blasted. Shot rattled on the roof shingles, screamed into the night sky. The Mormon pulled the second trigger and in the muzzle flash Guiana saw the man he knew must be Ben Stone, the smaller figure of Angelo. They were firing two-handed, down flat on the boards, part sheltered by the rails.

In a low crouch, Guiana started the long run for the gallery, his own six-gun blasting. He was aware of Curt Long to his right, Tonkin to his left, both men out of the saddle. In arrowhead formation, Guiana at the sharp end, they took the attack to Stone. And for one, exhilarating moment, Guiana thought they'd make it.

Suddenly, they were overwhelmed.

From outbuildings away to the right a second gun opened up, followed by two more from the nearest stand of trees. The thunder of hooves announced the arrival of Grit Harding and his partner, guns blazing. And as Ben Stone lunged to his feet, a cry of triumph ringing out, Curt Long let loose a desperate yell.

'The barn! Make for the barn!'

It was the closest building, in the only direction not blocked by men with blazing six-guns. As Long's yell was drowned in the roar of gunfire, Guiana raced after the sprinting Ranger, hoped to hell the big constable was close behind. It was thirty yards, no more, but hot lead was flying and men thwarted were screaming in rage.

Thirty yards, twenty, ten . . .

Long hit the big doors with his shoulder. They creaked, groaned, moved a foot — and jammed. Then Guiana piled into them. He went in with a flying sideways leap, felt his shoulder crack as he hit the heavy boards. The door grated, moved, swung open. Blackness loomed. Guiana staggered into the sweet-smelling gloom, turned to face a yard alight with the dazzling flashes of detonating weapons. Hoarse rasping breath and a groan of agony announced Tonkin's arrival.

'Get 'em shut!' Long gasped.

Together they struggled to swing the heavy door back. A man was pounding across the yard. As the gap between the two doors narrowed he snapped a shot, then a second. Breath hissed between Long's teeth. Then Tonkin's shotgun roared. The man screamed as shot tore into his chest and he was slammed backwards off his feet. Before he had hit the dust, the doors crashed shut. The beam dropped with a thud into iron brackets.

And, as if at a signal, every gun ceased firing.

★ ★ ★

'What the hell are they doin' now!' John Guiana said, restlessly prowling.

'Nothing much.' There was the sound of cloth ripping as Tonkin swept back his coat and tore open his shirt. 'Stands to reason there's no point in wastin' good shells when the men they're gunnin' for are trapped inside a barn with only one way out.'

Alongside him, Curt Long slipped a dusty bandanna from around his neck and used it to fashion a pad for the weeping wound in the constable's shoulder. Guiana offered his as a strapping to hold it in place, and with a sigh approaching satisfaction Tonkin buttoned up his shirt and muttered his thanks.

'I guess here's that proof you've been needing,' Guiana said from the shadows.

'Thank the Lord!' Tonkin said with deep feeling. His boots rustled through the straw as he crossed to the big blood bay, ripped open gunny-sack fastenings and riffled through crumpled bills. 'It's a pleasure to know I was wrong, but I get a kinda shivery feeling at the back of my neck at the thought I near hanged an innocent man.'

'Thank Curt Long, and put it behind you,' Guiana advised. 'Then, if you want *my* undyin' gratitude, come up with an idea for gettin' us out of here.'

'One thing's for sure,' Long said, 'if we don't come up with something pretty quick they'll rush us with all guns blazing, or soak the walls in coal oil and burn us out.'

'No sign yet,' Tonkin said. He'd moved to the door and with his face pressed to the timber was squinting though a crack in the weathered boards. 'Bunched up over by the house. Them three *banditos* plus Harding and his pard and Stone with Krane and that Mex hostler he seems fond of. Makes eight in all — '

'You're forgettin' you downed one,' Long cut in, and the constable chuckled.

'No, sir. I'm sayin' there's eight of 'em, but I'm not sayin' they're all up on their feet.'

'Seven, then,' said Long. 'For them that's better'n two to one odds.'

Tonkin spat. 'Each of us is worth two of them no good varmints.'

In the sudden silence, Guiana said, 'The true odds're seven to one. You two can walk out of here any time; this is between me and Stone.'

'Maybe once it was,' Tonkin said. 'But there's a Texas Ranger here spent time ridin' line while he got the goods on Stone, a humble constable who don't take kindly to bein' made a fool of by a Mex' hostler and three no-good bandits.'

Feeling a surge of emotion at this show of solidarity, Guiana watched him turn and again press his face to the door, saw the sudden stillness in the big man.

'Trouble?'

'Somebody moved fast. I counted seven. Now I see four.' He swung away, said to Long, 'You worked here, was I right sayin' there's only the one way in and out of this barn?'

'There's doors swing out the front of the loft, but down here — '

A splintering crash spun him around, chopping off his words. From the darkness at the back of the barn a gun spat flame. The blood bay squealed. Dark shapes kicked huge holes in the dry boards and came in with the cool night air, lunging from the shadows. Guiana drew and fired. A man roared, hit the wall with a thump and slid into the straw. A black Stetson rolled.

Then the 'breed was closing. No more than a dozen feet away, a black-gloved hand fanned the hammer of his six-gun. His lips writhed in a snarl of rage. His lean frame was as taut and as bowed as spring steel. Edging along the other side of the barn Cruz, the Mexican, was triggering his Winchester. Teeth gleamed white under the black moustache. He fired recklessly. Hot led whined, hissing past Guiana's head, punching holes in the barn's walls.

Silently, Tonkin went down, sliding to sit stiff with his back rigid against one barn door, a leg doubled and leaking blood. But he was ramming cartridges into the scattergun, forcing them in with teeth-clenched curses, swiftly swinging the shotgun up as the hammers snapped back.

Ghost-like, Curtis Long had slipped away.

A wild slug from the Mexican's Winchester seared Guiana's ribs like a red-hot branding iron. He sucked breath through his teeth, snapped a shot at the moving bandit, saw him slammed back against the wall. Sombrero knocked askew, Cruz struggled to lift the drooping long gun. Guiana's second shot took him in the throat. He went down gurgling in a red shower of blood.

On the far side of the barn, Con Shipley was up on one elbow. He blasted a shot that clanged off a bucket, screamed out through the roof. The next ripped the six-gun from Guiana's hand. He dropped to one knee, scrabbling for the fallen pistol with numb fingers — glanced up to see Sharpe Eagan grinning down on him, the gloved fist that had pounded his flesh now loaded with a cocked six-shooter.

Then, out of the shadows, the Texas Ranger opened up.

He took Con Shipley with a single aimed shot that flopped the wrangler onto his back, eyes staring sightlessly. Lightning-fast, Eagan whirled away from Guiana and threw himself sideways. Instead of taking him in the back, the Ranger's slug shattered the 'breed's left arm. He grunted with shock, staggered, dropped to his knees. At the same instant, Guiana's hand closed over his fallen pistol. Curt Long emerged warily from the shadows —

And both barn doors exploded inwards.

18

The drum of hoofbeats became muted, faded into the night.

'Let him go!'

This was Stone, but his words were wasted, for among the men left standing there was none who would have chased Sharpe Eagan.

'He'll make the border, and good luck to him,' said Brad Krane. 'But what about Long?'

'He is one slippery *hombre*, that Ranger,' Mig Angelo said.

'Too darn slippery for my liking,' Ben Stone said. 'But until he makes his move, what we've got is one town constable who's lost interest — and the man I've been huntin' for twenty years.'

'Get Tonkin to town,' Guiana said, 'or he'll die. You want that, Stone?'

'What I want is you stretching a rope,' Stone said. He chuckled. 'I think that can be arranged.'

They were gathered in the yard. The heavy barn doors had slammed open, knocking the wounded Tonkin groaning on his face, and for the second time Guiana's pistol was jarred from his grip as the timbers cracked his elbow. He rolled, face twisted in pain, saw Long's hand lifted in warning before he again melted into the shadows as Angelo and Krane sprang in through the open doors. He sat up, shaking feeling back into his arm, saw Stone and Harding ten feet away in the moonlit yard. Then Krane's six-gun had prodded him to his feet, and with a sick feeling in his heart he knew he was finished.

'Why?' said John Guiana now. 'Do I know you, Stone?'

'No more than I know you,' Ben Stone said, 'and I never set eyes on you in my life.'

'So . . . what the hell is this about?'

'It is about a mistake,' Mig Angelo said.

'A mistake I'll remember until the

day I die,' Stone said. 'It's about a young Mexican who saved my life, an owlhoot who left town ahead of a posse — '

'Harding's posse?' The question was jerked unthinking from Guiana, and he flicked a glance at the Crossing marshal then quickly shook his head. 'No. Not that. But where, then?'

'Nuevo Laredo,' Angelo said. 'Remember, John, I tol' you I am wanted for murder?'

'Krane,' Stone said, 'go get a rope.'

'Bring one of them horses,' Grit Harding said.

And from the gallery beyond the tall tree there was a soft gasp of horror.

'Jenny, go back into the house.'

'No. This time you've gone too far — '

'You heard me!' His voice cracked like a whip.

'Yes,' she said. 'And you heard me, though you chose not to.'

'You're upset.' He glanced across to where she stood in the deep shadows of the gallery, shook his head irritably. 'We'll talk later, when this is finished.'

'Can it ever be finished?' she said, and there was a break in her voice.

Stone deliberately turned his back. With a shrug, a shuddering breath heard clearly by Guiana, the woman went inside. Stone watched Krane emerge from the barn leading Cruz's horse and said, 'Every time I see a rope I remember you, Guiana,' and his hand lifted and with a flick of his wrist he whipped the bandanna from around his throat.

'The sight of rope burns might be shocking if I didn't have advance warning,' Guiana said, as he gazed impassively at the scars on the older man's neck.

With another swift movement, Stone removed the pearl-grey Stetson. His shock of white hair fell over his forehead. He brushed it back, studied Guiana.

'In those days,' he said, 'I had dark hair like yours. Too much like yours, as it turned out. You and me, we were in

Laredo at the same time, never saw each other, never knew each other except I knew you by reputation. When you pulled a bank robbery — '

'I remember that,' Guiana blurted.

'I was . . . I was spending a long hot afternoon with a beautiful woman.'

'My sister,' said Angelo. 'With my approval.' For some reason this was for Guiana.

'I guess I wasn't thinking.' Stone shook his head at the memory. 'You'd left town, but the *rurales* lost the trail, figured you'd swung back towards town, maybe never even left. They came hammering back in just as I left Angelo's adobe, looking too much like you, riding a horse too much like yours . . . '

'Yes,' Guiana said, his own mind busy with more recent memories, 'it must have been like that to put such a deep imprint on your mind.'

'So they hanged me just to be on the safe side — that's the way the *rurales* work and to them I was just another *gringo* — were leaving me to die real slow only a skinny Mexican sharp-shooter took out the *generalissimo*, or whatever the hell they call the boss, and in the uproar heaved a man choked half to death across his saddle and somehow made it clear out of town and into the hills.

'And now it's over. After too many years. Maybe I planted that tree in front of the house and watched it grow tall knowing it would come to this, but you'll hang from it, and this time there'll be nobody to cut you down, this time — '

The bullet took him in the back.

For a long second, Ben Stone stared at Guiana, but from the instant the pistol cracked from the gallery of the house his eyes were glazing. He went down in a heap, and somewhere to one side a man swore softly. Then Guiana was moving, twisting, stabbing a hand for his holster, his eyes as he whirled registered Mig Angelo with his old Sharpes up and level, Brad Krane dropping the lass-rope to make his draw, the six-gun in Grit Harding's left hand, and the savage light of triumph in the marshal's glittering black eyes as he prepared to relieve hours of frustration with a single shot.

But the shots that cracked viciously were not his, nor Harding's. A lean figure emerged from the yawning shadows inside the barn. The first shot from the the Texas Ranger's Winchester punched through Grit Harding's vest an inch below his badge and he crumpled soundlessly into the dust. The second took Krane between the eyes as he spun to face the new danger. The rangy foreman was dead before his knees buckled.

'No!' Guiana yelled.

He stepped forward, a hand lifted to stay the third shot that would have removed Mig Angelo from the fray.

A wisp of gunsmoke trailed from the muzzle of the Winchester as Long jogged across the yard.

'I could have taken Harding and Krane,' Guiana said, and he heard the resentment in his voice, wondered at it. 'This way,' he said, trying to rationalize, 'I've been dragged out of the mire without effort on my part — and that's wrong, ain't it?'

'This way,' Curtis Long corrected, 'an officer of the law has resolved a dangerous situation, an innocent man come out of it without a stain.'

'All right.' Guiana nodded, almost swamped by a sudden flood of relief. 'But Mig Angelo . . . ?'

'Bodies need buryin'. After that, it's not far to the border.'

'The woman.' Guiana took a breath, glanced towards the empty gallery, thinking back through the years. 'It took a woman to get me out of this, and I should thank her.'

'She was helping herself, not you. And if we don't stop jawin', there's a lawman in the barn who won't make it through the night. There's a buckboard by the house, horses in the corral. Come on, Johnny Guiana, let's take Joe Tonkin to town and get you home.'

We do hope that you have enjoyed reading this large print book.

Did you know that all of our titles are available for purchase?

We publish a wide range of high quality large print books including:
Romances, Mysteries, Classics
General Fiction
Non Fiction and Westerns

Special interest titles available in large print are:
The Little Oxford Dictionary
Music Book, Song Book
Hymn Book, Service Book

Also available from us courtesy of Oxford University Press:
Young Readers' Dictionary
(large print edition)
Young Readers' Thesaurus
(large print edition)

For further information or a free brochure, please contact us at:
Ulverscroft Large Print Books Ltd.,
The Green, Bradgate Road, Anstey,
Leicester, LE7 7FU, England.
Tel: (00 44) **0116 236 4325**
Fax: (00 44) **0116 234 0205**

In the one-horse town of Medicine Bluff two men were dead. Sheriff Jack Starr didn't need the badge on his chest to spur him into tracking the killer. He had his own reason for seeking justice, a reason no-one knew. It drove him to take a journey into the past where he was to discover something else that was to add even greater urgency to the situation — to stop Montana's rivers running red with blood.